the Book of Life

The Book of Life

MOVIE NOVELIZATION

Adapted by Stacia Deutsch
Based on the screenplay written by Jorge R. Gutierrez & Doug Langdale

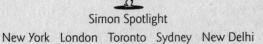

Simon Spotlight
New York   London   Toronto   Sydney   New Delhi

This book is a work of fiction. Any references to historical events, real people, or real places are used fictitiously. Other names, characters, places, and events are products of the author's imagination, and any resemblance to actual events or places or persons, living or dead, is entirely coincidental.

SIMON SPOTLIGHT
An imprint of Simon & Schuster Children's Publishing Division
1230 Avenue of the Americas, New York, New York 10020
First Simon Spotlight edition September 2014
THE BOOK OF LIFE ©2014 Twentieth Century Fox Film Corporation and Reel FX Productions II, LLC. All rights reserved.
All rights reserved, including the right of reproduction in whole or in part in any form.
SIMON SPOTLIGHT and colophon are registered trademarks of Simon & Schuster, Inc.
For information about special discounts for bulk purchases, please contact Simon & Schuster Special Sales at 1-866-506-1949 or business@simonandschuster.com.
Designed by Nicholas Sciacca
The text of this book was set in ITC Goudy Sans Std.
Manufactured in the United States of America 0814 OFF
2 4 6 8 10 9 7 5 3 1
ISBN 978-1-4814-2351-9 (pbk)
ISBN 978-1-4814-2352-6 (eBook)

CHAPTER 1

It was a quiet, calm morning at the large museum. The parking lot was filled with school buses. Children were inside the building, busy checking out the detailed historical displays and listening to stories about the past.

Thomas, a seasoned tour guide, was waiting outside, holding up a sign for his next group. He glanced at his pocket watch, then at the road. His group hadn't arrived yet.

Moving to the front of the museum steps, Thomas raised his TOUR GUIDE sign and whistled to himself until he saw a big yellow blur coming his way. It whizzed around the corner, tires squealing.

"Last tour of the day," he said to himself. "I wonder why no one wants them—" The school bus skidded to a halt with such force that Thomas jumped back. "Oh boy . . . ,"

Thomas muttered, noticing that one of the bus windows was splattered with spitballs. Then a spitball hit Thomas in the face.

"Bull's-eye!" a goth kid, dressed entirely in black, said.

Thomas wiped his face in horror.

The kids laughed as they poured out onto the sidewalk.

Thomas took a step back. The kids looked like trouble. The goth kid led the way with shaggy purple hair and spiked wrist bands, followed by a black-haired girl named Jane, who quickly roller-skated onto the sidewalk. Sanjay, a confident, cool-looking kid stepped up next with a sigh, along with Joao, a blond-haired boy wearing a strange top hat. Behind them all crept Sasha, and though she hardly looked threatening with her big eyes and blond hair full of bows, Thomas wasn't about to let her innocent look fool him.

"Hiiii!" Sasha giggled, clutching a doll tightly to her chest.

"A lame museum? Again?!" Sanjay whined.

"I hate stuff," said the goth kid.

"Yeah, me too," Jane added. The other kids nodded in agreement.

Thomas sighed. It was going to be one of *those* days.

Out of nowhere, a woman arrived at his side. Her name was Mary Beth. She was young, pretty, and eager to help.

"It's okay, Thomas. I'll take this group." Mary Beth looked at the kids with a mischievous smile.

Thomas squinted at her. "Um . . . are you sure? These are the *detention* kids." Suddenly, another spitball hit him in the face. He made his decision. If she wanted the kids, they were hers.

Mary Beth smiled. "Don't worry. I can handle them. You go take your break."

"Thank you!" Thomas said, smiling gratefully as he dashed back inside the museum.

The goth kid winked at his friends, then shot three massive spitballs at Mary Beth.

Mary Beth struck a pose and quickly deflected them with her TOUR GUIDE sign like a ninja warrior. She smiled confidently, spinning the sign. On the back it said FOLLOW ME.

"Follow me, kids," she said.

"Huh?" the kids said in unison.

The kids glanced at each other, then shrugged. Reluctantly, they started up the stairs toward the museum doors, but Mary Beth turned them away from the massive entry.

Sanjay said, "Yo, lady. The museum door is that way."

"Yes, it is," Mary Beth told him. "But you aren't like the other kids. No, no, no. You need to see something special."

She called the kids closer and pointed to the wall. "Right through that door!"

The kids stared at the blank wall, muttering together, "Huh?"

Jane stepped up. "You're seein' things, lady."

"Am I?" Mary Beth asked her. "Or are you *not* seeing things?" She took a step backward and disappeared through the wall.

"Whoa!" The kids were shocked.

"Come on!" Mary Beth reappeared. She held out her hand and a small ornate door appeared.

The kids considered the Aztec carvings in the wood, then followed her inside.

CHAPTER 2

"Today is November second. Does anyone know why that date is important?" Mary Beth asked as they worked their way down a narrow, dark, and cold hallway.

The kids all called out guesses. "'Cause it's Taco Tuesday!" cried Sasha.

"No."

"Ran out of Halloween candy day?" Jane said.

"Nope. Today is the Day of the Dead!" said Mary Beth.

"Is that like National Zombie Day or something?" goth kid asked. The kids all started to giggle.

"Come on, let me show you."

Jane stayed close to Sanjay. Suddenly, a security guard stepped into their path. All the kids jumped back in fright. The bearded man was skinny and his eyes shone hollow as he lit his face from under his chin with a flashlight.

"You can't go this way!" he roared.

The kids screamed.

Mary Beth stepped into the glow of his flashlight.

He said, "You will get us both in trouble. Ancient rules, of the, uh . . . museum administration."

Very gently, Mary Beth took his face in her hands and smiled at him.

The guard sighed and his voice softened. "Well, I suppose I could turn a blind eye, my dear."

She kissed him on the cheek. Blushing, he moved aside to let the children pass, but not without one last fright. He glared at Sasha. She screamed and ran after the others.

A moment later Mary Beth led her group into a large space. "Behold, children, the glorious beauty of Mexico!" She flipped a switch and enormous windows opened. Light spilled into the room, revealing tightly packed, colorful displays of Mexican folk art. The art lined the walls and reached to the ceiling with paper flags, flowers, and skeleton floats.

The kids gasped at the glorious sight.

Mary Beth moved aside, allowing the children to explore. There were Mayan and Aztec sculptures, papier-mâché monsters and skeletons, huge sombreros, woodcarvings, and colorful funny paintings.

"This place is loco!" Jane exclaimed.

"So many skulls," Sanjay said.

The goth kid wasn't going to be fooled into actually liking a museum. "At least that part isn't lame," he said, looking over Sanjay's shoulder.

Grasping her doll tightly, Sasha walked up a small staircase and looked up. "Whoaaaa." In front of her was a giant mural of a Mexican Tree of Life. At the base of the painting, there was an ornate book on a carved pedestal. Sasha called to Mary Beth, "What is this amazing book?"

"Ah, that is the Book of Life!" Mary Beth told her.

"It's so beautiful," Sasha gushed.

"All the world is made of stories and all of those stories are right here." Mary Beth opened the large book so that the children could see. "This book holds many truths." She flipped to a page titled "*Cinco de Mayo.*" There was an image of a wood-carved Mexican soldier with a sweeping mustache. "Some are actually true!"

Sasha asked, "The Battle of *Cinco de Mayo*?"

The goth kid exclaimed, "I love mayo!"

They all laughed.

Mary Beth smiled. "And some, not so much." She flipped to another page titled "*Chupacabras.*" There was an illustration of a small monster eating an entire goat in one gulp, then spitting out a perfect skeleton.

The goth kid exclaimed, "*El chupacabra*, the legendary goat sucker! I have to get one."

"Ewww!" Jane gagged.

Mary Beth moved quickly through the book's pages until she reached an ancient map of the universe. As the kids stared at the map, it was as if they were transported through the Milky Way and the solar system to Earth, and finally to Mexico.

"Although you may doubt some of these stories, there is one thing we know for certain: Mexico *is* the center of the universe." Mary Beth pointed at the center of the map, where golden rays of light shone down on a little island city.

"And long ago, in the center of Mexico, was the quaint little town of San Angel," she said as the light moved to reveal an illustration of Ignacio, a wooden figure wearing a giant sombrero, pushing a churro cart in the festive town square. The magical image showed San Angel, the Land of the Living.

"Churros! Churros!" Ignacio called out. Just then, a bird pooped on his cart. Ignacio considered the poop, then announced, "Frosted churros!"

Mary Beth said, "Naturally, since San Angel was the center of the universe, directly below it lay . . ." She paused as the map dipped to reveal the Land of the Remembered. The illustration now showed a captain with his hand raised, as flower petals floated up through glistening spotlights.

"The Land of the Remembered," Mary Beth told her tour group. "A festive and magical place for those who live on in the memories of their loved ones." She frowned as the memories turned dark. "And below that lies the Land of the Forgotten. The sad and lonely destination for those poor souls who are no longer remembered." The book showed a quick glimpse of a desolate wasteland, raining ash. An illustration showed a sad black skeleton fading to dust.

Mary Beth pointed to the branches on the Tree of Life mural behind the book. The kids looked up.

"But before I can properly begin our story," she told them, "you need to meet the two magical rulers of these lands." She directed them toward an image of a woman with a beautifully painted face. The lady was surrounded by all kinds of animals looking up at her adoringly.

Eyes wide with curiosity, Sasha asked, "Who is that?"

"That is La Muerte," Mary Beth explained. "She is made out of sweet, sugar candy."

The goth kid muttered, "She's so pretty."

"She is, isn't she?" Mary Beth replied. "She loves all mankind and believes that their hearts are pure and true."

Mary Beth gestured to an image of a skeleton with a white beard, wearing a regal black cloak and holding a cane that looked like a two-headed purple snake. Crying skeleton dogs serenaded him. "And that is Xibalba. That charming *rascal* thought mankind was not so pure, just like him."

"He looks spooky," Sasha said nervously.

"Yes," Mary Beth told her. "He's made out of tar and everything icky in the whole world."

"He's so pretty," the goth kid said about Xibalba.

The kids turned to him awkwardly and giggled.

"Let me show you something else." Mary Beth had them turn toward a small chest across from the Tree of Life mural. The chest was full of intricately carved wooden figures. "See, all of these wooden figures here—they represent real people in our story. Just like you and me."

"Whoa." The kids were interested in hearing more.

"And so our tale begins," she said. "On the day the people of Mexico call the Day of the Dead, or *el Día de los Muertos.*"

CHAPTER 3

Day of the Dead celebrations were under way in San Angel. The streets were filled with music and people wearing skeleton costumes.

In the cemetery mariachis played, women danced, and children laughed as families decorated their loved ones' gravestones for the holiday.

Mary Beth said, "On this festive, enchanted day, families bring food and offerings to the altars of their beloved."

"So, is Day of the Dead every year?" the goth kid wanted to know.

"Yes," Mary Beth answered. "But on this particular November second, the mischievous Xibalba had had enough."

*****

In the San Ángel cemetery, two graves lay side by side. One was aqua blue and full of lit candles, flowers, bread, offerings, and fruit. The other grave was old, gray, and cracked with weeds. It was spooky and appeared to have been forgotten.

La Muerte and Xibalba appeared, one behind each gravestone. They were arguing.

"Really, my dear," Xibalba was saying, "you have no idea how cold and vile the Land of the Forgotten has become."

"Ha! Just like your heart, Xibalba," La Muerte replied, echoing, "Just like your heart."

Xibalba wandered through the cemetery, causing candles to blow out at nearby graves. La Muerte followed him, relighting the flames. Though they walked among the celebrations, the two godlike figures were invisible to the people in the cemetery.

Xibalba sighed. "Why must I rule a bleak wasteland while you enjoy the endless fiesta in the Land of the Remembered? It's simply unfair." He never wanted to be stuck in the Land of the Forgotten.

Xibalba reached out toward an old man arranging flowers on a nearby altar. He was about to touch the man when La Muerte slapped his hand down.

"Xibalba!"

"What?" He shrugged. "It's his time. More or less."

La Muerte shook her head. "Not today, my love."

Xibalba stopped in front of her. "Come on, my dear, trade lands with me. I beg you."

"Ohhh." She laughed. "You're so cute when you beg."

"I'm serious," Xibalba moaned. "I hate it down there!"

"Hey! You're there because you cheated." La Muerte frowned. "You made your bed with that wager." She gave him a sad look. "You're not the man I fell in love with all those centuries ago."

"Let's not dwell on the past, *mi amor*." Xibalba quickly changed the subject. "Anyway, I was thinking, how about another little wager?"

"You think another bet will calm the flames of my anger?" She paused. "What exactly did you have in mind?"

"Let's check out the menu for the evening," Xibalba told her.

La Muerte turned herself into flower petals and let the wind carry her away. Xibalba melted into a puddle of black tar and sank into the earth. He reappeared next to her in the church bell tower that overlooked the cemetery. After a moment, Xibalba spotted the perfect scenario.

"Ahh. Look there, my love." He pointed into the distance. "The classic mortal dilemma. Two boys, best friends no less . . ."

La Muerte finished, ". . . in love with the same girl." She took a closer look at a little boy named Manolo, who was playing his guitar for a little girl named Maria. Manolo was a kind and gentle boy who loved music. His friend Maria was beautiful, courageous, and had a fierce fighting spirit. Maria smiled at her friend, but just as he was about to serenade her, another little boy named Joaquin leaped from the bushes, wooden sword in hand. Joaquin was strong, fearless, and loved to flaunt his fighting skills in front of his two best friends.

"Fear not, señorita," Joaquin announced, wearing a fake mustache. "Your hero has arrived!"

Maria giggled. "Is that so?"

"How dare you interrupt a *guitarrista*!" Manolo strummed his guitar with passion.

Joaquin was playing, pointing his sword in Manolo's direction, but Manolo dodged him gracefully, like a bullfighter.

"The girl is mine!" Joaquin announced.

Manolo chuckled. "Never! She is mine!"

Suddenly, Maria jumped between them, knocking them both to the ground. "I belong to no one!"

"Whoa!" The two boys looked at each other. Maria was even more awesome than either of them imagined.

Maria rolled her eyes at them and laughed.

In the tower above, Xibalba turned to La Muerte. "I believe we have our wager. Which boy will marry her?"

La Muerte agreed. "Very well. We will each choose one of these boys as our champion."

They glided down to the cemetery, transforming into an old man and old woman as they walked. The cemetery was crowded and no one noticed.

"Let's go wish them luck." Xibalba grinned, confident that his boy, Joaquin, would win the girl's heart.

CHAPTER 4

"Maria, weren't you grounded?" Manolo asked. He was holding his guitar, strumming the beginning of a song he was writing.

"My father is overreacting," Maria told him. "How was I supposed to know chickens don't like baths?" Just then, a chicken walked by blowing soap bubbles.

Joaquin stood to the side of the conversation, flipping swords in each of his hands. "Don't worry, he knows a real man is protecting you tonight."

"You're not even close!" Maria chuckled.

"But I have a mustache!" Joaquin said, wrinkling the fake mustache on his upper lip.

Manolo snorted. "Yeah, just like your grandma!"

Maria slapped Joaquin on his back, causing his mustache to fall off.

He set the wooden swords aside to grab the mustache. They all laughed, but then Maria's and Manolo's fathers interrupted the moment.

"Maria!" General Posada shouted, his voice echoing down the street.

"Manolo!" Carlos called his son.

Manolo and Maria rushed off, leaving Joaquin standing there alone, knowing that he didn't have a father to call for him.

Manolo found his father standing with his great-grandmother next to his mother's grave. He paused.

"Come, *mijo*." Carlos, who was dressed, as always, in a bullfighter's costume, beckoned Manolo closer.

Manolo lit a candle and placed a loaf of bread on the small altar to his mother, Carmen Sanchez. Beyond her gravestone were the stones for all the other Sanchez ancestors. The candles Carlos had lit for each one of his relatives flickered like stars.

Carlos placed a hand on Manolo's back. His thick black mustache wiggled as he spoke. "Your mother would be so proud of you."

Grandma Sanchez agreed. She had seen a lot in her time—she was Carlos's grandmother and Manolo's great-grandmother. Her wheelchair was next to Carmen's grave, where she could sit, watch, and knit.

"You think she'll come back tonight?" Manolo asked his father.

"Carmen is here," Grandma said surely.

Carlos agreed. "But it's more like a warm feeling you get when loved ones are with you." He motioned toward all the other people in the cemetery celebrating their loved ones. "All of these families have lost someone. But, as long as we remember them, we can feel their presence with us for one night each year."

As he spoke, all through the cemetery faint images of skeletal family members appeared, happily visiting the living. Manolo and his family couldn't see them, but they were there.

"Carmen will always watch over you," his father said.

Manolo remembered a time when he was with his mother in a lush flower garden. She was sitting in the sunlight, humming a lullaby. "She always smelled like flowers," Manolo said. "I remember her singing . . ."

"She was a good woman, that one," his great-grandmother said.

"I miss her so much." Manolo lowered his eyes and fought back a tear.

"Just be still, and you can feel it," Carlos assured him. "Your mother is here, along with all our ancestors. As long as we remember them, they are with us. The moment we forget them, they are truly gone."

Manolo closed his eyes. Images of Carmen and the ancestors swirled around him. "I can feel them," he said, and Carlos smiled.

An old woman approached the family at the gravesite. It was La Muerte, still in her disguise. "Kind people, may I please have a bit of your bread? I am so hungry."

Without even thinking, Manolo handed her the whole loaf. "I'm sure Mama would want you to have it. Right, Papa?"

Carlos's mustache turned up into a grin and he nodded. La Muerte smiled back.

"Thank you, my dear. In return, you have my blessing: May your heart be always pure and full of courage," she said.

"What do we say, Manolo?" Carlos asked his son.

Manolo didn't need the reminder. "Thank you, señora. Thank you."

Joaquin, wearing his fake mustache, watched the old woman walk away from Manolo and Carlos. "Ah, Manolo. Always giving away stuff for free. Right, Dad?" He turned and saluted the lavish altar set before the large, ornate mausoleum of his father. Captain Mondragon was a decorated war hero.

Back in the museum, Mary Beth filled in a detail for the story. "Joaquin's father, Captain Mondragon, had passed away fighting the fearsome bandit known as Chakal."

In the cemetery Joaquin heard a noise inside the mausoleum. He whipped out his wooden sword, leaping forward. His mustache was blown away by a gust of wind. Suddenly, an old man stepped forward into the light. Joaquin jumped back.

"Who's in there?" he called.

"Young sir, may I please have some of your bread? I'm so hungry," the man asked, frail hand outstretched.

But Joaquin wouldn't give away his father's offerings that easily. The old man would have to earn it. "This bread is for my father. And it's delicious!"

The old man, Xibalba in disguise, held out a golden medal toward Joaquin. "Perhaps you would consider a trade?"

Joaquin scoffed at the idea "An old medal? Please." He took a bite from the bread.

"Oh, this is no ordinary medal, my boy," Xibalba said. "As long as you wear it, you cannot be hurt, and it will give you immeasurable courage." When he passed it to Joaquin, the medal began to glow.

"Really? Deal!" Joaquin handed over the bread.

"But keep it hidden," Xibalba warned. "There is a bandit king who would stop at nothing to get it back." A sinister light shone in his eyes.

Joaquin looked at his father's grave. "Bandit king? You mean Chakal?" He turned back to the old man, but he was gone. "Where did he go?"

Back in their true forms, Xibalba and La Muerte met in the church bell tower above the cemetery. La Muerte was fixing a flower in her hair.

Xibalba did not tell her he'd given Joaquin the medal. He said, "So then, if my boy marries the girl, I will finally rule the Land of the Remembered."

"And if my boy marries the girl, you will—" She reached out and touched Xibalba's beard.

At first he enjoyed the attention, but then her hand grew

tight and she yanked on his beard. "You will stop interfering with the affairs of mankind," she demanded.

"What?" He was shocked. "I can't do that! Come on, it's the only fun I ever get."

She shrugged. "Then the bet is off."

Xibalba knew there was no arguing. He gave in. "Very well, my dear. By the ancient rules, the wager is set."

At the moment they shook hands, a great crash of thunder rattled the cemetery.

In the museum Mary Beth placed the wood figure of Maria between Manolo and Joaquin and said, "And so the greatest wager in history began. Manolo versus Joaquin for the hand of Maria."

CHAPTER 5

The children stared at Mary Beth with wonder.

The goth kid could barely believe the story. "Wait, so these ancient gods picked three little kids to, like . . ."

". . . represent the whole world?" Sanjay finished.

"Yeah, pretty crazy, right?" Mary Beth said.

The goth kid wanted more. "Yeah, keep going, lady!"

With a small nod, Mary Beth continued from where she left off.

Manolo, Maria, and Joaquin were running through town, enjoying the day. Suddenly, Maria heard a pig squeal. She stopped and spotted the most adorable little fellow locked behind the walls of a large corral. He looked at her with big pig eyes.

"You're so cute!" she exclaimed.

A knife-sharpening sound made her turn. She immediately noticed the butcher shop sign. Her eyes darted from the pig to the sign and back to the pig again.

"Oh no, not on my watch." Maria pulled out a wooden sword and announced, "We have to free the animals!"

"Huh?" Manolo and Joaquin said at the same time.

She gave them her best troublemaker grin. "Come on you guys, let's do this!"

"Hold on, Maria! Don't!" Joaquin wasn't sure.

But Manolo was ready. "Yeah!"

Maria lowered the sword on the corral lock, and with a crack the door swung open.

In the center of town General Posada was presiding over a military recruitment program. His trained soldiers were there to help. The townspeople gathered around in the public square to hear General Posada's speech. Carlos was watching the event along with Father Domingo and several nuns.

"People of San Angel, please, I beg you!" the general said. "After the revolution, we need more volunteers to join this mighty brigade."

The soldiers standing there were weak and pathetic. Their wood faces were full of tiny holes, as if termites had

had a feast. One wheezed violently and sawdust poured out of him just before his arm fell off.

A nearby orphan grabbed the arm and hurried away. "Woo-hoo!"

The general's face fell at the sight of his raggedy troop, but he straightened his sombrero and finished his speech. "A heroic brigade to protect us from Chakal." He unfurled a wanted poster with a picture of Chakal's menacing face.

The townspeople shouted out in fright. No one volunteered to join General Posada's troop.

Suddenly, the ground beneath them began to shake.

Ignacio, the boy who had the churro cart, exclaimed, "Oh no, Chakal is here!"

But it wasn't their fearsome enemy. Instead it was a stampede of crazy animals, bursting through the square like the running of the bulls in Pamplona!

"FREEEEEDOOOOM!" Maria led the animals' escape, riding the back of a pig like a horse.

Manolo, holding the pig's tail, was dragged behind, while Joaquin ran alongside, trying to keep up.

Maria waved her small sword and cheered.

The crowd panicked, and the general's soldiers instantly held up their hands in surrender.

"Maria! What have you done now?!" her father bellowed.

"Freedom is coming through!" Maria replied.

"Stop!" General Posada ordered.

Just then, Manolo lost his grip on the little tail. As he tumbled away, Joaquin tripped over him and they both crashed into the general, knocking him to the ground. The two boys kept flying through the air until they hit a fruit stand. Fruit rolled everywhere, and in the chaos, Manolo's guitar was trampled.

"Oh no! It's the crazy warthog!" an old man shouted.

Joaquin sat up and saw the warthog about to charge into General Posada. He leaped up, shouting, "Look out, General!" In a brave move, Joaquin knocked the general out of the way just in time. Joaquin was now in the warthog's path. The warthog slammed into him, sending Joaquin skidding on the ground for several feet.

To his surprise, he got up without a bruise or scratch. Joaquin noticed the glow of the old man's medal hidden under his vest and smiled. It worked.

One of the nuns, Sister Ana, was now in the warthog's path. "Oh dear!" she shouted.

Joaquin called to Manolo, "No retreat?"

Manolo replied in turn, as they had done so many times before, "No surrender!" He grabbed a woman's red shawl and placed himself between the nun and the warthog.

"*Toro, toro.*" With a bullfighter's skill, Manolo swiftly deflected the hog.

The townspeople began to cheer with shouts of "Olé!"

Carlos watched his son at work. "He has the gift," he said proudly to an old man standing nearby. The old man nodded as the fight between Manolo and the hog continued.

"Olé!" the crowd shouted again.

Carlos couldn't stop grinning. "Great form, *mijo.*"

Manolo leaped off a soldier's shoulders, using the shawl to parachute in front of the doorway of a shop. He shook the red shawl at the angry warthog, calling, "Hyah."

The warthog charged at Manolo. Manolo spun the shawl and teased the hog until finally, the warthog crashed into the shop.

"Olé!" shouted the townsfolk when they saw the warthog was stuck.

"That's my son!" Carlos said.

The old man smiled as the town hooted and hollered for Manolo. The rest of the animals ran away and escaped.

Sister Ana said, "Thank you, Manolo," while the nuns sang out, "*Gracias!*"

General Posada had been knocked unconscious when he fell. He opened his eyes slowly. "Oh my," he said. "What did I miss?"

Joaquin helped him up. "You okay, sir?"

General Posada put his arm around Joaquin. "You have saved my life."

Manolo came rushing up, holding the baby pig Maria had seen earlier. "And I—"

"Shhhhh. Quiet, boy. I'm talking." General Posada cut him off.

"But I—" Clearly the general hadn't seen Manolo's bullfight or how he had saved Sister Ana.

"Quiet," the general ordered.

Manolo looked down sadly. The town square was a mess. Small fires burned. Barrels and carts were all knocked over. A pig was playing tug-of-war with a soldier over General Posada's sombrero, which was also on fire.

The general surveyed the devastation. "Whaaa—? That girl is in so much trouble."

Maria peeked around the corner of a building. "Uh-oh."

"MAAAAAARIAAAAAAAAAA ! ! !"

Riding her pig, wooden sword dragging on the ground, she approached. "I'm sorry Papa, it's just that I—" She stopped as she noticed something broken on the ground. "Manolo's guitar!" Maria gave an apologetic look to Manolo.

"Maria!" Her father's face was red with anger. "This

rebellious nonsense ends now! You are going to become a proper lady."

"Why?" she asked.

"Because I said so." That was that. "I'm sending you to Spain. The sisters at the Convent of the Perpetual Flame of Purity will straighten you out."

Manolo and Joaquin both exclaimed, "What?!"

"But Papa—" Maria began to argue.

"No, it is decided." General Posada frowned at her. "Now go home!"

Maria began crying and ran off with Manolo's guitar still in her hand.

General Posada turned to Joaquin and pointed to the statue of Joaquin's father, Captain Mondragon. "Joaquin, you are so much like your father. This town could use a new hero." He put his arm on Joaquin's shoulder. "Come, you are like the son I never had! My boy, your father was like a brother to me."

As they walked away, the baby pig jumped out of Manolo's arms and promptly peed on his foot. The towns-woman took back her shawl.

Manolo tried to follow Maria, but his father stepped in front of him.

"*Epa!* Where do you think you're going?" Carlos asked.

"He can't send Maria away!" Manolo said.

"Well, fathers do what's best for their children. Come along."

Manolo took one last long look over his shoulder, but Maria was gone. He sighed and followed his father away from the square.

CHAPTER 6

On the outskirts of town Carlos and Manolo stood on a high hill overlooking San Angel. The baby pig stayed close to Manolo's side.

Looking out at the town's bullfighting ring, Carlos said, "*Mijo*, I saw how you fought that beast. You made our ancestors proud."

Manolo glanced at his father. "You think Maria was impressed?"

Carlos grinned. "Maria and every girl in town!" Manolo smiled and Carlos went on. "People said I was the greatest bullfighter in our family's history. But, it is you, my son, who will be the greatest Sanchez ever! They will write songs about you!"

"And I will sing them!" Manolo said enthusiastically.

"Wait, what?" Carlos asked, confused.

"I will sing them?" Manolo echoed with less certainty.

"Son, music is not work fit for a Sanchez bullfighter."

"But I want to be a musician," Manolo protested.

"No," Carlos said. "You must focus. Your training begins at once. Your Grandpa Luis taught me when I was about your age."

"Wait, isn't that when that bull put you in a coma?"

"Ah, memories!" Carlos nodded. "My only son fighting angry, thousand-pound beasts! The family tradition continues."

"Yay," Manolo moaned as he and the baby pig set out toward home.

Mary Beth told the students, "And so the day came when Maria would leave to study abroad. The three amigos would be no more."

The train station was crowded with people who came to wish Maria farewell. A group of nuns sang, "Adiós, Maria."

"Adiós, mijita," General Posada said as Maria embraced him. "Write soon." Beyond his daughter, the general noticed

Manolo and Joaquin standing sadly to the side of the others. He excused himself, barely able to hold in the emotion. "I'm going to go over there."

Maria hurried to her friends. "I'm going to miss you guys," she told the boys.

"We'll be here waiting," Joaquin said.

"For as long as it takes," Manolo added.

Maria hugged Joaquin, then turned to Manolo.

"Don't ever stop playing, okay?" She held him for a long embrace.

Stepping back, she pointed a finger at Joaquin's chest. "And you. Don't you ever stop fighting for what's right."

Joaquin agreed.

Manolo handed Maria a box with holes punched in the top. "I got you a present. You should probably open it now."

Joaquin was stunned. "Wait a second, were we supposed to bring gifts?!" He hadn't brought anything.

Maria gave Joaquin a small smile, then opened Manolo's box. Inside was the adorable baby pig she'd rescued, all curled up and snoring softly.

"I named him Chuy. He'll look after you," Manolo said.

Maria tenderly lifted the little pig out of the box and snuggled with it. "Oh, I remember you."

"I figured you needed a little part of town to go with you," Manolo told her.

Maria was touched. "Thank you."

"Seriously, no one told me about bringing gifts," Joaquin groaned.

Maria turned to him and asked, "Can you hold Chuy for me?" She then picked up a box of her own and handed it to Manolo. "This is to make up for breaking your guitar."

In the distance a train whistle blew and the conductor shouted, "All aboard!"

The three friends' eyes all went wide. She was really leaving. Maria took Chuy and said, "I gotta go." She couldn't look at the boys or she'd start to cry. "Don't forget me." And with that, Maria hurried toward the train. The wind blew off her bonnet, which landed on the station platform.

"Maria! Your bonnet!" Joaquin gave chase.

Manolo knelt to the ground and opened the box. Inside was his guitar, completely repaired. On the side was engraved, ALWAYS PLAY FROM THE HEART. He couldn't believe it. He held the guitar close and looked out to the slowly moving train.

Maria sat sadly in her compartment, with Chuy asleep on her lap, when she heard Manolo's voice.

"Maria!"

She looked out the window. Manolo and Joaquin were running next to the train.

"When you come back, I will sing for you!" Manolo called out.

Joaquin ran faster, passing Manolo. He was holding up Maria's lost bonnet. "And I will fight for you!"

The train picked up speed, leaving them behind.

Maria leaned back and smiled to herself. Chuy snorted, then went back to sleep.

"It would be years before they would ever see Maria again," Mary Beth said. The children were quiet as she revealed to them what happened over the next ten years as the boys waited for Maria's return: Manolo unwillingly practiced bullfighting with his father every day—he wanted to play beautiful music, not face bulls in the ring. Meanwhile Joaquin trained to be a soldier with General Posada.

"One, two, three! One, two, three!" General Posada made Joaquin march away from a marbles game with Manolo.

Carlos kept Manolo so busy, he had to sneak away to play his guitar.

Joaquin marched past Manolo's hiding spot. "Hey, Manny!"

"March!" The general prodded Joaquin forward.

Once, while Joaquin was on a practice field, defeating other soldiers, Manolo watched from the hills above, strumming his guitar.

"Yes! Just like your father!" General Posada declared Joaquin the victor of the day.

Over at the bullfighting arena, Carlos looked for Manolo. Manolo ran in, just in time for his bullfighting lesson.

"And that's how you finish a bull!" Carlos said, proudly admiring his own handiwork. "With a fake bull."

Manolo was awkward and uncomfortable when he took the sword from his father. Carlos wrapped him in a matador cape, which made Manolo even more uncomfortable. He preferred to play music with his friends the Rodriguez brothers—Pablo, Pancho, and Pepe—who had formed their own mariachi band and understood Manolo's love for music. The tallest and oldest brother, Pepe, loved eating good food almost as much as he loved playing the violin. Pancho, the middle brother, had a scruffy beard, a big belly, and enjoyed playing the trumpet. Their youngest and shortest brother, Pablo, played the *tololoche*, a string instrument that sounded similar to the double bass.

But Carlos didn't like the mariachis—he thought they were a bunch of cowardly, lazy, out of shape goofballs, and he didn't want his son to pick up their bad behavior. So he tried to keep Manolo occupied with his matador training (and away from the Rodriguez brothers) as often as he could.

As Joaquin left San Angel to go to battle, Manolo sang with the Rodriguez brothers. His tune was cut short when his father arrived. Carlos grabbed Manolo by the ear.

"I will *not* wait for you," he said firmly.

"Papa, I was on my way!" Manolo tried to explain as his father dragged him through town, past several posters announcing a bullfight. The Rodriguez brothers chased along in tow.

Mary Beth explained what happened next. "After years of training, Manolo's father organized his first bullfight. And as luck would have it, it was on the day Maria returned. . . ."

CHAPTER 7

Manolo and his father were preparing for the big bullfight in the matador's chapel near the arena. Manolo's great-grandmother had come to support her great-grandson. She sat in her wheelchair, knitting, while Carlos helped Manolo dress.

"Ay, Manolo, playing all night with those mariachis?! You want to end up like those bozos?!" Carlos slammed the door on the musical Rodriguez brothers and locked them out.

"Okay, Manny. We'll wait outside," Pepe said, peeking through a small window.

"I don't think Mr. Sanchez likes us," Pancho told his brothers.

Pablo rolled his eyes. "Ya think?"

Carlos threw one of his swords across the room. It stuck into the wood near the brothers. "Quiet, you three!"

They ducked, then ran away.

Carlos put away Manolo's guitar. "You live under my roof? You live under my rules. You will be a matador!" He held up Manolo's cape.

"Papa, this is my life!" Manolo objected.

Carlos swept his hands toward the walls of the chapel. All around them were paintings of Sanchez matadors: strong, fierce-looking men. At the end of a row—after Carmelo, Jorge, Luis, and Carlos—there was a poster of Manolo looking bored.

"All the Sanchezes are bullfighters!" Carlos said. "Every. Single. One of us."

Grandma rocked in her chair. Even though she was more than one hundred years old, she was strong as rock. "I was a beast in the arena. A beast," she said, bragging about her own bullfighting skills.

"It's in your blood," Carlos told Manolo. "It's your destiny. How many times do I have to say it?"

"This is not *me*. This is *you*." Manolo picked up his guitar, ready to leave.

Carlos blocked his way out. "My son, Joaquin may be the hero of the town, but today you will be the hero of the ring." He raised a sword. "If for once you actually finish the bull."

Pepe's voice came through the window. "But he finished a bull the other day in practice!"

It was true. Manolo *had* faced the bull in the ring. "*Venga, toro—*" Suddenly, the bull was struck by lightning and fell to the ground, dead.

"That did no count," Grandma said, knitting needles clicking.

"No. Killing the bull is wrong," Manolo said.

Carlos sighed. "Here we go again."

"Kids today, with their long hair and their no killing stuff." Grandma shook her head.

"I'm out of here." Manolo pushed past his father to the door.

"Don't you love your family?" asked Carlos.

The question made Manolo stop. Grandma looked up. Manolo turned slowly around.

"Then go get that bull, *mijo*. Don't dishonor our name," Carlos said. "Just be a Sanchez!"

Without deciding what to do, Manolo left the chapel.

"*Mijo,*" Grandma said to Carlos. "He no gonna do it."

Manolo was alone in the tunnels behind the bullring when a voice called out to him.

"Hey, Manolo!"

Joaquin stepped out of the darkness, his medals gleaming in the light. "No retreat?"

Manolo gave a small smile. "No surrender!"

The two friends hugged.

"The hero of San Angel returns!" Manolo clapped Joaquin on the back.

"Ah, come on. You didn't think I was gonna miss your first little bullfight, did you?"

"And Maria's here too!" Manolo told him.

Joaquin beamed at the news. "Have you seen her? I can't wait to show her these babies." He brushed off the jingling medals on his chest.

Manolo pursed his lips. "Oh, so she's back only to see you."

"Come on, that's not—" Joaquin began when Manolo's face lifted.

"You have your medals, but I have the bullring. We'll see which Maria prefers." He was going to fight the bull after all.

"It's a good thing you're finally taking bullfighting seriously," Joaquin said.

"You should see me in the bullring. That's where I really do my thing now. A true Sanchez man." Manolo puffed out his chest and stood tall.

Joaquin put his arm around his friend's shoulder. "Those are some big shadows we live under, huh, buddy?"

Manolo had to agree. "Huge." He sighed.

Before walking away, Joaquin touched the medal that the old man had given him all those years before. He looked at Manolo and said, "Hey, brother. May the best man win Maria." He left Manolo in the tunnel.

Manolo stood for a moment, listening to the excitement of the crowd. Then he stepped forward into the light of the arena.

Mary Beth explained to the children what happened next. "In honor of Maria's return from Europe, the town received a rare visit from its most noble son: Joaquin, who was now a decorated hero. . . ."

Everyone rose to their feet as Joaquin entered the coliseum. As he walked, his medals clanked. He soaked in the applause, tossing his cloak dramatically on the ground.

"They say Joaquin goes from town to town saving them from bandits!" said an old man in the crowd.

Joaquin whistled for his horse, then leaped on its back

and rode it like a surfboard, waving at his fans. He signed autographs as the town soldiers chanted his name like teenage girls.

Above the crowds La Muerte and Xibalba watched their champions from atop the arena, hidden from the view of the townspeople. "Yes, that's my boy!" Xibalba cheered Joaquin on.

Joaquin jumped from his horse into the stands, walking up to General Posada. "Afternoon, my general. That is a mighty mustache you have."

The general began clapping, when suddenly, the whole stadium went silent.

Maria entered. She was all grown up now, wearing high-heeled boots that clicked as she moved toward Joaquin and her father.

Her face was covered by a fan, and her long hair flowed in the wind. Chuy, now a fully grown pig, hurried along at her side.

Mary Beth said, "As expected, everyone in town was curious to see how the young Maria had grown. . . ."

*****

A soldier declared, "The jewel of the town has returned!"

Everyone she passed stared at her with awe.

When Maria stopped to greet two orphans, Luka and Ignacio, Sister Ana told the other nuns, "And she's going to be helping at the orphanage."

One girl told her friend, "And I hear she reads books, like, for fun." She made a sour face.

"No!" her friend said in disbelief.

Ignoring everyone's whispered comments about her, Maria reached her seat.

Joaquin greeted her with a bow. "Señorita Posada."

Maria snapped back the fan, revealing her face. The whole crowd gasped at her beauty.

"*Hola*, Joaquin," she said, smiling.

The young girl in the stands said to her friends, "*Ahhh!* And she's so natural!"

An old man was so taken by her that his jaw fell open and his teeth fell out.

Above the arena, Xibalba gaped. La Muerte elbowed him hard, cracking his ribs.

"Ow! What?" He closed his mouth and looked away.

Pancho Rodriguez blew his trumpet, announcing Manolo was entering the arena. The crowd rose to welcome the next Sanchez matador.

"And they say Manolo might be the greatest Sanchez ever!" the old man said.

"Yeah! That's my boy!" La Muerte clapped wildly. Xibalba shot her a jealous look and crossed his arms. "What?!" La Muerte said.

In the ring Manolo looked up at Maria, but she covered her mouth with her fan. "I would like to dedicate this corrida to Miss Maria Posada," Manolo said, waving his cape in a rhythmic pattern. "Welcome home, señorita."

Maria wouldn't look at him—she thought that bullfighting was wrong and was disappointed in her friend.

But back in the ring Manolo didn't know what was wrong. As the time for the bullfight approached, he tried to convince himself he was ready. At least, as ready as he would ever be.

A side gate opened in the arena, and out ran the raging bull.

CHAPTER
8

This was no ordinary bull. The bull that faced Manolo was covered in skull tattoos. It was wearing spiked armor and had metal tips on its horns.

The Rodriguez brothers had followed Manolo into the ring. Now they took one look at the bull and fled for their lives.

"I'm allergic to dying!" Pepe shouted.

"Especially in the face!" Pancho covered his eyes. Pablo screamed.

"We got your back, Manny!" Pepe said as he jumped behind the ring walls.

Manolo glanced quickly at his father in the stands, then struck a pose, gripping his cape tightly. *"Venga, toro! Venga!"*

The bull charged.

"*Venga!*" Manolo gracefully whipped his cape aside as the bull passed by.

"Olé!" The crowd went wild.

"Now that's a Sanchez!" Carlos said proudly.

Manolo waved to the crowd as they threw flower petals into the ring.

Manolo picked up a red rose from the ground and raised it to Maria. She smiled at him.

"Manolo!" Maria warned as the bull charged him again.

Tossing the rose into the air, Manolo turned an easy back-flip out of harm's way. He landed, sliding on his knees like a rock star as he caught the rose in his mouth, flamenco-dancer style.

"Olé!" the crowd shouted again.

"That's my son!" Carlos was even more proud.

The orphans in the stands did the wave.

The bull was furious. He charged again, and this time Manolo pivoted in place, leading the bull in a circle around him. He moved his cape and the bull followed it. When the bull finally stepped back, his horns had written "Maria" in the dirt.

The crowd couldn't hold back their excitement. "Olé! Ma-no-lo! Ma-no-lo! Ma-no-lo!"

Maria was impressed by Manolo's gesture. Joaquin was jealous that Manolo was getting all the attention.

Manolo walked over to his father. Carlos handed him a sword. "Come on, *mijo*. For me. For our family. Be a Sanchez."

Manolo took the sword and walked slowly back toward the bull. The bull lowered his head, stomping and snorting.

The crowd went silent.

Carlos gripped a piece of the arena wall so hard it cracked. Maria's knuckles tightened around her fan.

Manolo took aim. He saw his reflection in the blade.

He also saw Maria's reflection.

"No." He shoved the blade into the ground. "Killing the bull is wrong!"

The bull charged. It passed within an inch of Manolo, blindfolding itself as it tore the cape from his hands. Blinded, the bull smashed into the arena wall and knocked itself completely out.

Everyone was speechless.

Carlos was disappointed.

Grandma said, "See? I told you he no do it."

The one person who mattered shouted for Manolo. "Bravo! Bravo!" Maria called out.

The crowd booed, but Maria clapped enthusiastically.

"Hey, we don't have to kill the bull!" Manolo tried to tell everyone.

Maria could see that this was not going to end well. "Oh no. Manolo." General Posada pulled her away from the arena.

Manolo watched them go, knowing he'd lost her—forever.

"Adiós, Maria," Manolo muttered as people began to throw their trash at him.

Someone tossed his guitar into the ring. It hit him in the head and he fell unconscious to the dusty ground.

A short while later Carlos shouted in his ear, "Manolo. Manolo! Get up!"

Manolo opened his eyes to find the arena was now empty. Grandma stood with Carlos, who was staring disappointedly at his son. "I'm sorry, Papa," Manolo said.

Carlos said, "Do not make it worse by apologizing! A Sanchez man never apologizes! Never!"

Grandma added, "Ever."

"If being a bullfighter means killing the bull," Manolo told his father, "well, then I'm no bullfighter."

"No." Carlos took the handles of Grandma's wheelchair.

"You are no Sanchez." He pushed her away.

Even the bull was disappointed. He rose, shook off the dust, and walked into the tunnel without looking back.

High above Manolo, in the top seats of the arena, Xibalba and La Muerte watched.

"Victory!" Xibalba said. "That poor kid never had a chance, my dear. Good game, though."

La Muerte wasn't giving up. "It's not over." She gestured to the bullring below.

Manolo picked up a rose from the ground. He tucked it into the top of his guitar like a microphone and began to play. It was a song about Maria and how much he adored her.

He didn't see Maria enter the stands, but La Muerte did. She smiled.

Maria looked on in awe as Manolo sang and played beautifully from his heart. When the song was finished, Maria let loose a heavy breath. "Ay, Manolo." She took a step forward, but her father called her name. She ran off knowing that Manolo never saw her.

Xibalba was confused. "What just happened?!"

La Muerte put a hand over her chest and said, "Ha! You don't know women, my love."

CHAPTER 9

Mary Beth told the children at the museum, "That night, General Posada threw a grand party to welcome Maria back. But, you see, he had bigger plans. . . ."

Maria sat at a table surrounded by all the high-ranking officers in the military, including Joaquin.

The soldiers toasted, "To Joaquin!"

And General Posada made a speech. "A great hero! Too bad you're just in town for a few days. If only there were something that would make you stay, like a special girl? Ey, Maria?"

"Papa!" Maria didn't like where this was headed.

General Posada grinned. "What?! What did I say?"

"Oh, my father." She laughed nervously, turning to Joaquin and teasing, "It's so wonderful to see you again, Joaquin. Look at that mustache!"

Joaquin jiggled his mustache, and his medals jingled together.

"And all those medals! What's this one for?" Maria reached forward to touch Xibalba's magic medal.

Joaquin jumped away. "What?! Nothing! Ah . . . why don't you tell me a little more about Europe?"

Maria pulled back her hand. "Ay, I loved it! Such beautiful music. And art. And books! It was wonderful."

Joaquin responded, saying, "Books, art, wonderfulness. You sound like you've learned so much, Maria. I'm sure one day you are going to make a man very, very, very happy. And I hope that man's mustache, or his medals, make you very happy."

Maria raised her eyebrows. "Oh, is that so?"

Joaquin sat up a little taller. "Well, yes. Behind every man with an amazing mustache is a beautiful woman."

"Oh yes. And I'll cook and clean for him and be at his beck and call." Her words were sarcastic, but Joaquin didn't notice.

"Uh-huh. That sounds so good. And you sound . . ." He stared at her, losing track of what he was saying. "You're just so pretty."

Maria tilted her head. "Are you kidding me?"

General Posada spewed his drink over the soldiers nearby. "Oh boy." He could see where this was headed.

"Is that how you see a woman?" Maria asked Joaquin.

Joaquin wasn't sure what had gone wrong. "Um . . ."

Maria's voice grew tight. "We are only here to make men happy?"

The soldiers nodded their heads in agreement. Joaquin was flustered at how this had gone wrong. "So, I don't know."

"I believe I have lost my appetite," said Maria. As she rose, the soldiers at the table stood with her. "No, please, stay seated." She waved them off. "Now, if you'll just excuse me, I must go check on Chuy. That's my pig. I need to spend time with someone civilized. *Buenas noches.*" She left the room in a huff.

When she was gone, a soldier whispered to Joaquin, "You've picked yourself a feisty one!"

Joaquin was in a terrible mood. Without even looking at the man, Joaquin punched him hard. "Good one, Joaquin! Very witty," the soldier said. General Posada shook his head at the turn of events.

*****

Manolo and the Rodriguez brothers wandered the dark and empty streets. Pepe played the violin, while Pancho played trumpet and Pablo played the guitarlike *tololoche*.

"I can't believe the general invited the whole town! Except for you, Manolo," Pepe said.

"Sorry, bro." Pablo tried to be supportive.

"He even invited us. And he hates us," Pancho put in.

"It's hopeless." Manolo's shoulders slumped with a long, tragic sigh. "I've lost her to Joaquin."

Pepe had an idea. "Listen, listen, all we gotta do is play the right song and, trust me, everything will turn around in the space of four bars."

Pancho gave a little laugh. "We've already been to four bars!" He added, "Twice!"

Suddenly, Pepe stopped. "Hold it. I know exactly what to play." He called the guys into a huddle and pulled Manolo into the circle.

"Okay, okay. It has to be romantic and classy," Pancho said after hearing the plan.

Pepe agreed. "But with tons of dignity!"

Maria lay on her bed, snuggling with Chuy, when she heard the music outside. She knew that voice. It was Pancho playing on a tiny toy piano below her window, and the song wasn't very good.

Chuy knocked a cactus off Maria's balcony at him to stop the racket.

Maria snuck near the window so she could see, but was still hidden in shadow.

Manolo was with Pepe. "Wow, that totally captivated her." He groaned.

Pepe shrugged. "I don't get it. That one always works!"

But Pepe had another idea. "Ooo, I got it! Follow my lead." Pepe danced and spun around to another equally bad song, ripping off his shirt to reveal a tattoo of himself on his chest.

Chuy threw another potted plant at him. Pepe fell to the ground, dazed.

"Ha! Very romantic, Pepe," Manolo laughed sarcastically.

Maria, still hidden in her room, covered her mouth while she giggled. Chuy growled, so she tugged him out of sight, where they could both find out what the boys would do next.

"Hey, that's all I've got, man." Pepe quit.

Pablo leaped forward. "Okay, my turn!" He prepared to sing. "One, two, one two *tres cuatro*!" But before he even hit the first note, a massive potted cactus landed on his head. "Time to eat our feelings!" Pablo muttered from inside the plant as he also quit.

The brothers ran off toward a restaurant. Manolo stood out on the street alone.

As Maria's lights went out, Manolo picked up his guitar. The engraving from Maria shone in the moonlight. ALWAYS PLAY FROM THE HEART. He closed his eyes . . . and began to play.

CHAPTER 10

Manolo began to sing a beautiful song that he'd written just for Maria. His music was pure and true, and each note was born from the long years he'd spent loving her from afar.

Maria moved back to the window. This time she opened the doors and stepped into the moonlight. She didn't want to miss a single word of the song.

Manolo spotted Maria above him. It spurred him to sing with even more fervor.

The farm animals and the townspeople were starting to pay attention as well.

La Muerte stood on a rooftop, grinning.

Joaquin heard the song too. He stood in the hallway outside Maria's room for a long moment, then had an idea. He turned around to go back to the party downstairs.

Pepe and his brothers hurried out of the restaurant to provide backup music for Manolo.

From a nearby rooftop Xibalba looked on in horror—he realized that he was going to lose his bet with La Muerte.

The Rodriquez brothers stacked themselves into a human ladder. While still singing and strumming his guitar, Manolo began to climb toward Maria's balcony.

The moon was full. Maria met Manolo under the stars. He leaned in slowly toward her lips. Both of them were lost in the moment, but at the last second Maria pulled back. "Did you think it was going to be that easy?"

Surprised, Manolo lost his balance and began to fall. He tossed Maria his guitar as he and the Rodriquez brothers crashed to the ground.

Wearing Pancho's trumpet on his head, Manolo sighed. "I—I kinda did."

Maria laughed as Manolo dusted himself off beside the heap of Rodriguez brothers. "Manolo!" she called. "Hold on, I'm coming!" But at the bottom of the stairs, she found Joaquin, standing with General Posada. Joaquin held out a small box with a ring.

"Joaquin! What are you doing?"

General Posada pulled Joaquin's leg to make him kneel. "Maria, um, will you . . . will you marry me?"

Maria's jaw dropped wide open. "Uhhhmmm."

Four pretty girls behind her shouted simultaneously, "Yes!"

Joaquin told Maria, "Don't worry, your father already said you could."

Maria's jaw dropped even farther. "He did what?"

"Who else could protect us from Chakal?" The general held up the wanted poster he always carried.

Maria stepped back from Joaquin, but the general pushed her forward. Just then, the door opened. Pepe carried Manolo into the room.

"Uh-oh," Pepe said as one of the girls at the party fainted.

Manolo, still delirious from the fall, put his arm around Joaquin. "What'd I miss?"

Joaquin was confused. "Wait, did he propose too?"

"No." Maria gave a small laugh and asked Manolo, "Were you going to?"

"Uh, what?" Manolo didn't have a clue what was going on.

"Well, I proposed first. So go fight a bull or something," Joaquin said.

Manolo pushed Joaquin away and the soldiers caught him.

Maria was angry. "You two are acting like fools!"

Manolo thought he was the victor until he saw Maria's face. "Wait, me too?"

One of the soldiers holding Joaquin was amazed at his muscles. "Oh, you're so strong, Joaquin."

"Thanks. I work out a lot," Joaquin said. With a smirk, he moved closer to Manolo. "Look, I love you, you know that, but how are you going to protect Maria if you can't even finish a bull?"

The most cowardly soldier said, "Good one, Joaquin."

"Oh yeah?" Manolo wasn't shaken. "You will never be as great a hero as your father."

Everyone gasped.

The soldier said, "Now, that's just uncalled for."

The fight got worse from there. Manolo pointed at Joaquin. Joaquin responded, saying, "Oh, you better get your finger out of my face," and poking his finger back at Manolo.

"Don't point at me!" Manolo shouted.

They started swatting at each other like little kids.

"I'm the best pointer you've ever seen!" Joaquin cried.

A soldier handed Joaquin a sword. He pointed it at Manolo. "En guarde, little brother."

"Manolo!" Pepe yelled.

Manolo turned, expecting a sword, but Pepe handed him

his guitar instead. Manolo gave Pepe a questioning look.

"What? You wanted a banjo?" Pepe asked.

Joaquin began to chuckle. "Ha-ha! Look at him! He's got his guitar. What are you gonna do?"

Manolo raised his instrument. "I'm gonna teach you some manners." He clanked Joaquin's sword with the neck of his guitar.

Maria'd had enough. She stepped between them and with some fancy footwork of her own, disarmed each of them within seconds. "Did I mention I also studied fencing?"

Manolo caught his guitar while Maria caught the sword. She tried to give Joaquin back his weapon, but he refused it. "Fine. We'll settle this later," Joaquin said.

"Any time. Any place." Manolo replied.

Maria shook her head. "Really, guys?"

Joaquin stormed out of the house. "No! Don't go Joaquin!" a cowardly soldier shouted after him.

As General Posada's dinner guests were settling back into the ballroom, the front door opened with a bang. The orphan boys, Ignacio and Luka, dashed inside.

"The *bandidos* are coming!" Ignacio announced.

The cowardly soldier began to shake in fear. "And Joaquin is gone!"

"All is lost!" the nuns sang. Everyone ran to hide.

CHAPTER II

Chakal's bandits scurried toward the town, while the townspeople hurried to lock their doors. Chato, Chakal's right-hand man and *bandido* lieutenant, cackled in joy as the town gate, covered with Chakal's wanted posters, exploded. The bandits entered San Angel, wearing barrels of TNT on their backs and carrying torches.

"Tremble in fear before the might of Chakal's army!" Chato said as his men burst through the smoke.

General Posada shouted above the chaos, "Women and children, go to the church! Men, we're going to drive Chakal's bandits off! Who is with me?"

He was met by silence as the soldiers fled in fear. General Posada let out a long breath. "*Ay!* This is not good."

The dastardly *bandidos* reached the center of town.

They were terrible to look upon, with their arms and hands made of metal. They smiled mischievously as they took in all the loot they could pillage from the town. Chato, their leader and the shortest *bandido*, stood on a central staircase and announced, "Listen up, you cowards! These are Chakal's demands." He rolled out a ridiculously long parchment scroll and put on reading glasses.

Chato read the list while the *bandidos* collected the goods from frightened townsfolk.

"Hand over your chickens, monies, bacon, jars, mustache wax . . ." He paused and squinted at the words. "Ah, this looks like 'jelly' but I think it's 'jewelry'. . . Yeah, jewelry!"

A thief called Mofles sadly gave back the jelly he'd taken.

Chato finished Chakal's demands. "Anyways, if you give all of this to us, then maybe we won't burn your town down."

Manolo drew his swords and approached the *bandidos*. He tried not to focus on the fact that there were at least thirty of them versus one of him. "You want the town? You're gonna have to go through me," he said bravely.

The four most menacing bandits moved toward him. A tall, skinny *bandido* named Cuchillo with a hook for a hand loomed over him, followed by Chato and Mofles. Then came Plomo, who had a spiked mace for a hand and was by far the biggest *bandido*. They lifted their weapons. Manolo stood taller. Plomo began to swing his mace, when a voice called out.

"Hey, ugly!"

The four bandits turned to see Joaquin high on a rooftop, sitting atop a white horse and wearing his father's sombrero. He looked like a serious hero.

"Why don't you fight a real man?" Joaquin challenged the bandits. "With a really awesome mustache!"

Joaquin's horse jumped house to house, until finally Joaquin leaped off his steed and into the air, performing a fantastic swan dive. He shouted his own name as he dove. "JOOOOOAAAAQUUUIIN!"

At the last second he somersaulted and landed between Manolo and the bandits.

"Thank goodness you are here!" General Posada was thrilled.

Joaquin stepped into the light like a superhero. His cape flapped in the wind. With a flick of his wrist, Joaquin took off his sombrero and tossed it to Manolo. "Here, hold this." Then he gave Manolo his cape. "And this." He handed over his swords. "And this. Oh, and if that's too heavy, maybe you can just hand it to Maria."

Joaquin winked at Maria. She rolled her eyes.

Joaquin turned to the bandits and said, "My name is

Joaquin, son of Captain Mondragon. Tonight, the town of San Angel is under my protection."

The bandits laughed at him.

"Prepare to be beaten." Joaquin put his hands on his hips.

Joaquin and the bandits looked at each other angrily.

"Get him, Plomo!" Chato ordered.

Plomo charged at Joaquin, swinging his mace like a madman, but Joaquin was fast. He snatched it out of the air and kicked Plomo away like a flea. Joaquin shouted his own name with each strike.

The other *bandidos* attacked. Joaquin didn't even sweat as he defeated them one by one.

The bandits kept charging, but Joaquin was strong and determined. The townspeople started chanting his name.

The nuns sang out, "Who wants some more?"

Chato was growing more and more angry. "GET HIM!"

His men charged as a pack. Joaquin didn't feel any pressure. He took a second to greet Maria, "Hey, girl."

"You goofball!" Maria shrieked.

All the bandits then jumped on him, pinning Joaquin to the ground. Chato punched him repeatedly.

Joaquin felt no pain. He laughed, saying, "Ow. Ooo. Oh. All right, that's just not hurting at all."

Suddenly, Chato noticed a glowing medal on Joaquin's chest. "The beautiful hero," Chato whispered under his breath. "He has the Medal of Everlasting Life!" The bandits looked at one another, stunned, but none of the other townspeople heard him.

Joaquin quickly covered his medal, got to his feet, and punched out all four bandits. He said his name, "Joaquin," as each man dropped to the ground.

Manolo, standing near the bandits, was blown back by the force of Joaquin's furious punches.

Joaquin stared Chato in the eye. The bandit leader stared back, then commanded his troops, "Retreat!" The bandits all ran off.

"And don't ever come back!" Joaquin shouted after them. The town was saved. Everyone celebrated.

"That was amazing!" Maria said, congratulating him on his victory.

Manolo was the only one who wasn't impressed. "Yeah, you really are a hero." He sighed.

"Perhaps now we possibly could continue our conversation, Señorita Posada?" Joaquin put an arm around Maria's shoulders.

She looked at her father and then at the people of the town; they were all waiting for her answer.

"Maria, please, do it for the town," her father said. "Without Joaquin, we're at the mercy of Chakal!"

Maria nodded silently, then went to Joaquin, leaving Manolo in the square.

Manolo could hear her as they walked away. She said, "So why don't you tell me more about how you got some of those medals. . . ."

Joaquin's voice became faint as he replied, "Well, I got this one for delivering a baby with one hand while arm wrestling a bear . . ."

"Well, duh. Of course she's gonna go with Joaquin! Did you see that mustache?" Sanjay pointed out.

"You crazy?" Jane asked him. "Maria is doing this to protect the town."

"Putting her duty before her heart," the goth kid added.

"Yes," Mary Beth told the kids. "Life can be really tough for the living."

Inside the matador's chapel Manolo was putting away his bullfighter's uniform. His father stood nearby, looking at an altar dedicated to Carmen. Grandma was knitting.

"Failing, in and out of the ring—the whole Sanchez family would be so disappointed in you," Carlos told Manolo.

"Please, don't say that." Manolo's throat felt like a huge lump was lodged inside.

Suddenly, his father pulled him into an embrace. "Listen. You love Maria? Then fight for her. Like a man!"

"It's too late. Joaquin proposed to her already." Manolo had no fight left in him.

"Now, that's a real man." Carlos admitted he admired Joaquin. In response, Grandma pelted him in the head with a piece of fruit.

"Quiet, Carlos!" She turned to her great-grandson. "Manolo, if Maria didn't say yes to Joaquin, then she said no."

Manolo mentally reviewed what happened in the town square.

"So what are you gonna do about it, son?" Carlos asked.

Manolo's eyes lit up. He kissed Grandma on the cheek and ran out into the night.

CHAPTER 12

At the museum Mary Beth explained, "Chakal, a beast of a man, once possessed Xibalba's magic medal."

"Chakal! Chakal!" Chato called as he ran into the bandits' hideaway, a skull-shaped cave in the middle of the desert. Most of the bandits were still sleeping when Chato and the others returned from San Angel.

Chakal sat in front of a small fire sharpening a massive machete. His face was hidden by the darkness. The floor was covered in coins and medals.

Chato rushed in and announced, "We found the medal . . . the Medal of Everlasting Life! It's in the town of San Angel—"

Like a massive, monster wolf, Chakal rose and pounced on Chato. Chato was pinned beneath Chakal's gargantuan strength.

"Medal! Are you certain?!"

Chato choked out, "I swear! I swear!"

Chakal picked up Chato to look him in the eye.

"A beautiful hero wears it to protect the town." Chato pointed at a dirty bedsheet with a picture of the medal crudely painted on it. "It looked just like that!" A small image of Xibalba disguised as an old man was drawn on the sheet too.

"Gather my men. We ride for San Angel." He then tossed Chato out of the cave.

Chakal stood in front of the medal painting. The fire lit his frightening face and illuminated his scars. He smiled a sinister grin and said, "You've come back to me, Medal."

It was still dark when Joaquin dropped Maria off at her front door.

Xibalba settled on a nearby rooftop to see his hero get the girl.

Joaquin was still talking about his medals. "I got this one for saving some orphans from a fire and going back in for their cribs and their toys. And then I saved a little puppy one time that had a thorn in its paw. And then I got this medal for saving the president—"

"Well, here we are!" Maria cut him off. "Thank you for this most informative talk—about you."

Maria just wanted the night to end, but Joaquin thought that he had finally won her over! He reached into his pocket. "I have something for you, Maria." He pulled out a photograph and handed it to her.

"That is so nice of you," Maria said as she took the gift. But she raised an eyebrow when she saw it was an autographed picture of Joaquin. "Wow. I'm speechless," she said sarcastically.

"Yeah, I know, right? I get that a lot." He leaned in for a kiss.

Maria turned her head away. "Good night, Joaquin."

That wasn't how he'd expected her to react. "Maria." He stopped her from going inside.

"Yes?"

Joaquin took off his sombrero. Underneath the hat, he had her old bonnet from the train station.

"You kept it all this time?" Maria was surprised at his sincerity.

"It's what kept me going," he said. When Maria smiled at that, Joaquin asked, "About my proposal—will you at least just think about it?"

Maria nodded. "Good night, Joaquin."

When she closed the door, Joaquin did a dance on her porch. "Yes! Yes, yes, yes! Joaquin, you're awesome!"

Xibalba did a little dance too. "Yes!"

Maria lay back on her bed. Chuy snuggled into the blankets. She set aside the picture of Joaquin and looked at an old picture of herself, Manolo, and Joaquin from the day she left town. It seemed so long ago. . . .

Click. A pebble hit her window.

Maria stepped out on her balcony to find Manolo below.

"Meet me at the bridge at dawn."

"I can't, Manolo. My father won't—"

"Please, Maria, I beg you," Manolo pleaded. Maria gave a little nod of agreement. Manolo smiled as he ran off into the night.

Xibalba held up his double-headed snake cane in the shadows as Manolo dashed by him. The eyes of the snake glowed when he struck the ground. The snake came to life.

"If she meets him alone I will lose the wager. Fix this for me, old friend," Xibalba said.

The snake slithered off, following Manolo.

CHAPTER 13

At dawn Maria hurried toward the floating bridge to meet Manolo. The bridge connected the island of San Angel to the Mexico mainland. The moon was fading and the sun began to rise.

Maria gasped when she saw that the pathway was covered with candles and flowers. At the top of the hill, a beautiful old tree was glowing with sparkling candles.

Beneath the tree Manolo stood, playing his guitar for her.

Maria tried to remain cool, though she felt overwhelmed by the amazing scene.

"This is what I wanted to show you." Manolo pointed toward the town. At that exact moment the sun broke through the clouds, hit the stained-glass church steeple, and illuminated the town like a glorious, magical jewel.

"It's so beautiful," Maria said.

"What you're feeling," Manolo told her, "that's how I feel every time I'm with you." He knelt down in the center of a circle of candles. "I can't offer you a ring. I have nothing to give but my love."

"Oh, Manolo . . ."

Manolo went on. "I may not be the town hero, Maria, but I swear with all my heart, I will never, ever stop loving you."

Maria touched his face and dropped to her knees in front of him.

"And I will never stop loving the man who plays from the heart."

It was a beautiful moment, until Xibalba's snake slithered out from the roots of the old tree.

"Snake!" Maria warned Manolo, but it was too late for him to escape the snake's sharp fangs. With a great shove, she knocked him out of the way. The snake bit her, instead.

Maria collapsed into Manolo's arms. "No!" he cried. "Maria!"

The snake slid back and disappeared among the roots of the tree.

"Help!" Manolo screamed.

*****

There was a boom of thunder before the rain began to fall. Joaquin reached the shoreline just in time to see Manolo walking through the downpour carrying Maria's body.

"What did you do, Manolo?" Joaquin asked.

Manolo could barely speak. "There was a snake and . . . she saved me."

Joaquin checked Maria's wrist for a pulse. "Maria."

The town began to gather behind him.

Choking on the words, Joaquin reported, "She's gone."

The entire town was in shock.

"Why didn't you protect her?!" Joaquin was furious with Manolo. The medal on Joaquin's chest began to glow and he reached for his sword, but before he could pull it out, General Posada came rushing forward.

"Maria! Oh no. Oh noooo!" The general gathered her into his arms before turning on Manolo. "This is all *your* doing! Leave, or so help me I'll . . ." His voice dropped. "My little girl . . . What have you done, boy? What have you done?!"

Manolo lowered his eyes. "It should have been me."

Joaquin agreed. "Yes. It should have."

Leaving the others to tend to Maria, Manolo took his sorrow and pain and walked away alone.

*****

In the museum the kids looked up at Mary Beth with tears in their eyes.

"No! Maria died?" Sasha couldn't believe it.

"That can't be right!" Sanjay said.

"What kind of story is this? We're just kids!" Even the goth kid was upset.

Mary Beth was sad too. She told the children, "As the sky cried with rain, Manolo went back to retrieve his guitar."

The rain poured down. The candles had all gone out. Steam and smoke rose, creating an otherworldly feel.

Manolo found his guitar in the dirt. He knelt to get it, sighing. "I will never see her again."

Xibalba, in his old-man disguise, came up behind him. "Are you certain?" Lightning revealed the old man's true identity. "You want to see Maria again?" he asked.

"With all my heart," Manolo replied.

Xibalba discarded his disguise and transformed into his ancient godly form. "Think about what you say, boy."

A crash of lightning revealed a skull shape in Manolo's face. He looked at the words on his guitar. He knew what he wanted. "With all. My. Heart."

"Done." Xibalba snapped his fingers and the snake

returned from beneath the tree. Manolo was startled when suddenly, the snake's two heads bit him hard.

"Maria." With her name on his lips, he fell lifeless to the ground.

The kids in the museum gasped.

"No! Manolo too?" Sanjay asked.

The goth kid said, "What is it with Mexicans and death?"

Mary Beth knelt down to hear Sasha say, "But, it can't end like this. Can it?"

Mary Beth put her hand on Sasha's little head and said, "Oh, my sweet child, death is not the end."

CHAPTER 14

Manolo woke up next to the same tree he'd fallen beside. "Where am I?" he murmured. His guitar was nearby. It all seemed so normal, until he reached out his hand and discovered—he was a skeleton!

"Huh? Whoa!" He turned his head to see the Land of the Remembered—a festive, vibrant place alive with beauty, music, and magic.

The streets were full of happy skeletons going about their business. Manolo stood on a hill above the city. He watched the skeletons below for a moment, then a hot air balloon floated up to greet him.

A skeleton riding a skeleton horse leaped out of the balloon. The Land of the Remembered captain said, "Welcome to the Land of the Remembered."

"I made it!" Manolo was pleased.

The captain said, "And on the Day of the Dead, no less."

"Where . . . Where is . . . ," Manolo said, confused as he reached around to find his guitar.

The captain said, "You're going to be a little disoriented at first. Don't try to take it all in at once. Let's start with your name."

Then Manolo remembered. "Maria Posada!" Manolo said.

The captain checked for Maria's name on his clipboard. "Really? Parents and their crazy baby names. There's no Maria Posada on my list."

"No. I'm looking for Maria Posada," Manolo explained.

"Oh," the captain said, waiting for him to reveal his name.

"My name is Manolo Sanchez."

"Another Sanchez?" The captain took a good look at Manolo. "Man, that family just keeps growing."

This was good news. "My family! They'll help me find Maria! Can you take me to them?"

"I'd love nothing more than to reunite a young couple!" The captain made room on the horse. "Just hold on."

Manolo gripped his guitar in one hand and the horse with the other as they started to gallop. "Whooooooaaaaa!"

*****

Mary Beth explained to the children, "The Land of the Remembered was vibrant and joyous! Everything was like the land above, but it was more colorful, it was more beautiful, it was more festive! And on the Day of the Dead, the place was bursting with parties and parades."

The horse stopped on a long bridge. Manolo looked out at a spectacular parade passing down the street.

"There, your family is in that one," the captain said.

"Whoa." Manolo's eyes were wide.

"Get in there!" The captain shoved Manolo off the bridge.

Manolo flew through the air.

A giant bullfighter skeleton on an intricately decorated Aztec float caught him. "Oh yeah. Another Sanchez bullfighter!" he said, setting Manolo on his feet.

"You are the amazing Carmelo Sanchez!" Manolo exclaimed in awe.

"Yes. I was famous for fighting bulls without a cape!" Carmelo bragged. To show just how amazing he was, Carmelo tossed his cape on the ground and spit on it.

Manolo had to admire his ancestor's courage, but he was on a mission. With no time to waste, he asked, "Can you help me find Maria Posada?"

"La Muerte can help you. She helps everyone. Hold on." A massive bull-shaped piñata came toward them. Carmelo knew to dodge it, but Manolo didn't. The piñata hit him full force. When it snapped open, an avalanche of candy carried him away.

His ancestor cried, "Wait for me, little Sanchez. I take you to La Muerte!"

Manolo crash-landed on the plank of a parade float that looked like a Spanish ship from 1492. He looked up to discover a conquistador bullfighter had conquered the remains of the piñata bull.

"The great Jorge Sanchez!" Manolo recognized the man.

"At your service! I was famous for fighting bulls with only one arm and one leg!" Jorge showed Manolo his skill.

Manolo laughed. Jorge took a good look at his relative and asked, "You're Manolo, the one who plays the guitar?"

Manolo shifted his guitar into his other hand, saying, "Yeah. That's me."

Jorge got a dreamy look on his skeletal face. "You know, when I was younger, I always dreamt of singing in the opera."

That was a surprise. "You did?"

Jorge nodded. "But as you know—"

Manolo and Jorge recited their fathers' echoed words. "Music is not work fit for a Sanchez bullfighter."

Jorge said, "The same story." They shared a sad moment.

Manolo asked him, "Can you take me to La Muerte?" Before Jorge could answer, Carmelo leaped down onto the end of the plank. Manolo flew up as if launched from a catapult.

"He's new," Carmelo told Jorge with a shrug.

"He reminds me of me. But less handsome," Jorge replied.

Manolo landed on a parade float that looked like a bullfighting plaza. In the middle of the float, three massive bull piñatas were spinning in the breeze.

Manolo immediately recognized the next fighter from his family. "Of course! It's Luis 'El Super Macho' Sanchez."

Luis bowed. "I was famous for fighting three bulls at once!" He spit in three different directions and stabbed three bull piñatas with a sword. Each piñata exploded with candy.

"Grandpa! It's me, Manolo." Manolo rushed forward to hug Luis while Carmelo and Jorge arrived on the float.

Luis took a long look, then grinned widely. "Manolo! I'm so happy to see you." Then he slapped his grandson's cheek. "Why did you disgrace the family name?! Playing the guitar?! And you couldn't finish one bull? You were a clown!"

A Sanchez family clown, riding a bike and wearing makeup, honked his horn.

"Sorry, cousin Chucho," Luis apologized, putting an arm around Manolo. "Welcome home, *mijo*." He pointed to a parade float ahead of them. "Your mother will be very happy to see you."

Manolo gasped. "Mama?"

The float was shaped like a round pyramid with dancing skeleton girls on every level. Atop the pyramid was Carmen, dancing by herself.

Manolo's face hurt from smiling so hard. He leaped to the top of the pyramid. Carmelo, Jorge, and Luis followed. When Manolo reached the top, Carmen stopped dancing.

"Manolo?"

It was as if time stood still. The parade sounds and music faded away.

"Mama!"

Mother and son embraced.

"Manolo!"

CHAPTER 15

"I missed you so much." Manolo didn't want to let his mother go. He hugged her hard and held on.

"*Ay, mijo*, it's been like a hole in my heart. I've waited so long for you." She suddenly pushed him back. "But not long enough! What are you doing here?! It's too soon!"

Manolo explained, "I'm here to be reunited with the love of my life. You are going to love Maria, Mama."

Carmen softened. "I'm sure I will. *Ay*, Manolo, you look just like your father. So handsome you turned out!"

"And I became a bullfighter, just like you wanted," he told her.

"Me? Are you crazy?! Haven't you learned anything from your family's history?"

"What? But Dad said—"

Carmen was angry. "That Carlos, wait till he gets down here!"

She turned Manolo around to where a group of their ancestors had gathered. He waved to them all.

"Now come on, *mijo*." Carmen made the introduction. "Everyone, this is my son, Manolo."

The bullfighters rushed to embrace him. Two tough cousins, the Adelita twins, shook his hand and said at the same time, "Hey, *primo*."

"Being with the whole Sanchez family and you, Mama. This is incredible," Manolo said.

Carmen's float stopped at the base of a tree-shaped castle in the center of the land. "This is La Muerte's castle."

"I don't see it." Carmelo was facing backward. Jorge set him straight. "Oh."

"Savage," Jorge muttered.

Carmen put her arm around her son's shoulders. "Come, she will help you find my new daughter-in-law."

The two massive doors opened and Manolo and his family entered the castle. Glass skeleton chandeliers illuminated the front hall, and the ceiling was covered with paper flags and streamers. The family stepped on a floating bridge headed toward La Muerte's throne room.

"Whoa! It's so pretty," Carmelo said.

"Now, this is a castle!" Luis added.

"We were always her favorites," Jorge said. "You know how bullfighters flirt with death, eh?"

Carmen moaned. "And that's why there are so many of you down here. La Muerte's throwing a big Day of the Dead fiesta for everyone."

Carmelo walked along a table of food, snatching everything he could grab.

Jorge pulled a dish out of Carmelo's reach. "Animal!" he cried.

At the end of the long table, a figure sat with its back to Manolo and his family.

Carmen gave her son a nudge forward. "Ask her, *mijo*."

Manolo said, "My lady, could you help me find Maria Posada?"

"Who are you calling lady, bullfighter?" The figure turned. It wasn't La Muerte. It was Xibalba. The Sanchez ancestors around Manolo gasped and backed away in fear. "The Land of the Remembered has a new ruler. Who you ask? Little old me."

"You again!" Manolo exclaimed.

"But La Muerte would never hand her domain over to you," Luis said nervously.

Xibalba rudely belched. "She lost a bet."

"Oh. She would do that." Luis nodded.

"This land is finally mine, all thanks to you, Manolo!" Xibalba grinned.

"What?" Manolo hadn't a clue what he meant.

"Well, La Muerte bet that Maria would marry you. I bet that Maria would marry Joaquin. And since you're not around anymore . . . Maria is going to marry Joaquin just to, you know, protect her beloved town." Xibalba glanced up, toward the Land of the Living. "So I win."

"But Maria passed away. I saw her . . ." He began to realize what had happened. "Oh no."

"Oh yes. . . ." Xibalba laughed.

Manolo fell to his knees. Luis put his hand on Manolo's back and asked, "*Mijo*, what is it?"

Xibalba began to brag about the trick he'd played.

When Maria lay lifeless on her bed, Joaquin came to visit. He leaned down and let his medal brush against her arm.

"One snake bite merely put her in a trance. My champion easily woke the sleeping beauty," Xibalba boasted.

The medal glowed. Maria's eyelids fluttered, and abruptly, she sat up, gasping for air.

"Oh my goodness! It's a miracle!" General Posada cheered.

"Thank you!" The nuns sang and crossed themselves

while Father Domingo looked on proudly.

"I'm . . . I'm . . ." Maria started to say.

In the land below, Manolo finished for her. "Alive."

Xibalba raised a glass from the grand table to make a toast. "Cheers!"

Manolo considered what he now knew. "One bite? Your snake . . . It bit me twice! You cheated!" He was so angry that Luis and Carmelo had to hold him back from attacking Xibalba. "You will pay for this!"

Xibalba stood and walked across the tabletop. "In all my years, no one, in any realm, has ever talked to me like that and survived." He spread his mighty wings and loomed over Manolo, flashing hundreds of sharp teeth. "So I ask you— are you threatening me, boy?"

The Sanchez ancestors were afraid, but not Manolo. "I will expose you to La Muerte. And then you and I can settle things!" he exclaimed.

"You'll never reach her in her new realm. I should know, I rotted there for eons." Xibalba flicked his flinger, flinging Manolo back into his family. "Now, if you'd all excuse me, I have a wedding to plan. Ciao!" He burst through the ceiling and disappeared.

*****

Back in San Angel, Carlos knelt in front of the tree where Manolo had been bitten. There was a poster of Manolo and a humble altar made of flowers and candles, plus a little broken guitar.

"Ay, Manolo . . . ," Carlos said sadly. "There are so many things I wish I could have said to you."

Meanwhile, in Maria's bedroom, Joaquin sat on the edge of her bed.

"What happened?" Maria asked him. "Wait . . . where's Manolo?"

The others looked away, so Joaquin answered, "I'm sorry, Maria. Manolo passed away."

"No!" she stood, but unable to find her feet, stumbled. "It can't be . . ."

Sister Ana caught her. "I'm sorry, dear."

Joaquin held her while she sobbed.

General Posada said, "Maria, we're all sorry Manolo's gone, but Joaquin just saved your life. You see, he will always protect you."

"General, this is not the time." Joaquin tried to stop him.

But General Posada ignored him and moved Maria to a quiet corner of the room. "Please, for everyone's sake, *mija*. Make him stay."

Maria looked to Joaquin. He was clearly ready to leave

town to seek out and fight Chakal.

"Will you stay in San Angel if I marry you?" she asked him.

Joaquin nodded, knowing it was wrong. "Yes, but you don't have to—"

"I accept Joaquin's proposal," she told her father.

Joaquin couldn't believe what he'd heard. He vowed he'd stay and make her happy.

Outside the window, Xibalba sighed. "Ah. Young love."

Manolo couldn't let Xibalba win. "I have to find La Muerte!" He begged his ancestors, "Please, please, help me."

They gave each other nervous looks.

Carmen said, "*Mijo*, stay here with us."

"No more worries!" Luis said.

"Epic fiestas every day," Jorge added.

The Adelita skeleton twins put in, "With the whole Sanchez family."

Carmelo slammed into Jorge. "And all-you-can-eat churros!"

Manolo looked at his family. This was hard, but he knew where he belonged. And it wasn't here. Not yet. "Thank you, guys. But I need to be with Maria. It's all I've ever wanted."

At the museum, Jane asked Mary Beth, "How's Manolo going to get back?"

The goth kid couldn't believe it. "He's stuck there. Forever! And Maria is going to marry Joaquin."

"All right, do you want me to continue?" Mary Beth asked, then waited until they settled down. "So, one thing was for sure, Manolo needed help from his family."

"If La Muerte is where Xibalba rotted away . . . ," Carmen started.

"Then she's in the Land of the Forgotten," the Adelitas finished.

Carmelo shivered. "Oh no, oh no."

Jorge elbowed Carmelo, saying, "Quiet, you!" He turned to Manolo. "There's only one way to get to the Land of the Forgotten—through the Cave of Souls."

Luis said, "Going there would be certain doom."

Everyone looked worried. But not Manolo. He looked up with a fierce grin, saying, "It's a good day for doom."

*****

The entire family cheered and waved to Manolo, Carmen, and Luis as they rode off on skeleton horses into the sunset. Manolo felt tough and ready for victory.

"He's a Sanchez, I tell ya! A Sanchez!" Luis said.

"You know this is impossible, right?" Jorge asked Carmelo.

Carmelo smacked Jorge on the back, then kept waving. "Hey! Good luck, little Sanchez!"

There was hope in the air as the three skeleton Sanchez adventurers rode across the Land of the Remembered.

"The legendary Cave of Souls was rumored to be at the edge of the Land of the Remembered," Mary Beth told the children. "Many had tried to reach it, but none had ever returned. At least, not in one piece."

CHAPTER 16

Luis, Manolo, and Carmen approached the Mountain of Souls. They went as far as they could on horseback, and then had to walk.

The mountain rose before them like a Mayan pyramid. A grand waterfall plummeted out of the sky, down to the surface of the mountain where towering steps led to the mouth of a huge stone skeleton head. The whole thing glittered in gold.

"*Caramba*, it hurts just looking at it." Luis turned away his eyes.

The climb looked impossible, but there was no other way in. One step at a time, the group slowly made their way toward the cave entry in the skeleton's mouth.

"Are we there yet?" Luis asked. No one answered, so

every few feet he'd ask it again. "Hey, are we there yet? Are we there yet?" He didn't stop asking—until they were there.

Around the cave's mouth were the crushed and broken bones of those who had tried to enter in the past and not survived.

"We made it, *mijo*." The bones didn't scare Luis. Manolo and his mother looked at the bones, then at each other. Luis asked, "C'mon! What are you guys waiting for?"

He rushed forward a few feet when—*WHAM!*

A huge wall shot up from the ground, obliterating Luis and sending his bones flying in all directions. The giant skeleton head came to life. The Guardian of the Cave roared, "You are not worthy!"

Luis's head sailed by Manolo and Carmen before landing on the ground.

"Hey! My arthritis is gone!" Luis announced happily.

"Grandpa!" Manolo hurried to help.

Suddenly, a crack formed in the ground and quickly spread toward Carmen and Luis.

"Mama!" Manolo sprinted toward his mother as she snatched up Luis's head. Carmen and Luis jumped out of the way just in time. But the force of the earthquake sent Manolo skidding backward as the ground opened around him.

"Manolo!" Carmen shouted.

Walls shot up all around Manolo, trapping him in an enormous labyrinth.

"Face the labyrinth and earn the right to be judged!" The guardian's voice echoed.

Carmen and Luis were above, looking down at Manolo in the maze. The earth began to rumble again, releasing three huge boulders that rolled toward him. Manolo sprinted through the maze, trying to outrun the massive boulders.

"I can't see him! Lift me up!" Luis told Carmen. She raised his head above the labyrinth walls so he could see where Manolo was going. "I see him!"

Just then, a hole appeared in the ground and swallowed Manolo. He fell several feet down, straight toward a row of deadly spikes, but managed to use his guitar as a prop to stop himself in time.

"Where did he go?!" Luis couldn't see him any longer.

Manolo pulled himself back up from the pit, inch by inch, until he saw the exit to the maze.

But then Luis said, "Uh-oh."

"What? What's happening?!" Carmen asked in a panic.

"It's okay, honey. He's totally okay," Luis reassured Carmen, then told Manolo, "Run for your life!"

Manolo took off for the exit, but those massive boulders

were close on his tail. Manolo was nearly free, when a new wall rose in front of him, blocking the exit. With no other option, he turned to face the boulders.

Using a trick he'd learned as a bullfighter, Manolo swished past the first boulder as if he were fighting a bull.

He flipped over the next two boulders, and when the third one came back at him, he managed to use the three together as steps to get out of the way. He landed safely on the other side. The boulders crashed into each other and shattered.

Manolo looked to Luis and Carmen and took a bow.

"That was so beautiful," Luis gushed proudly.

But the danger wasn't over. The ground began to shake again and the labyrinth floor lifted to Carmen and Luis's level.

Manolo was ready to face a new threat, until he saw what was coming. The giant skeleton head of the cave rose, revealing an entire skeleton body. Manolo stepped back. This was the Guardian of the Cave in all his glory, and getting past him was going to be harder than anything Manolo had faced so far.

The guardian raised an enormous obsidian sword high above his head, preparing to strike. "You have earned the right to be judged."

"*Ay, ay, ay!*" Luis's skull said.

"For. Maria." Manolo said, and he closed his eyes.

"Manolo!" Carmen cried.

The Guardian of the Cave swung his sword with a mighty roar.

Miraculously, the obsidian sword shattered into a million pieces the instant it touched Manolo. The skeleton was shocked. That was unexpected.

"Manolo Sanchez, your heart is pure and courageous," the guardian said.

Carmen ran to her son and hugged him.

"You and yours may enter," the guardian told them, lowering down to let them enter.

"Ay, mijo!" Carmen hugged Manolo once more, then she slapped him. "Don't do that again."

Manolo smiled at his mother and Luis's head, then led the way into the cave.

It was dark in the Cave of Souls, darker than a starless night. Manolo pulled out the two swords he'd brought along and raised them for protection.

"This is the Cave of Souls?" Luis asked.

"Grandpa! Show some respect!" Manolo shouted a warning as a shadowy figure rose behind them. Manolo,

Luis, and Carmen braced themselves. The ancient being was shaped like a giant bell, with a beard made out of clouds. His skin appeared like clear wax with a warm inner glow. Draped in a series of long robes with symbols from various ancient cultures, the Candle Maker carried an ancient leather-bound book.

It was the Book of Life, the very same one Mary Beth showed the children in the museum.

The solemn situation quickly turned comical as the Candle Maker became very animated. This guy was clearly not a threat. "That was awesome, man! The giant boulders were like, pew! And you were like, swish! Swish! Swish! And then the Cave Guardian, he came in and was all—" He acted out what had happened outside with each phrase. Imitating the guardian's voice, he shouted, "I'm going to judge you with this giant sword!"

"Excuse me, sir!" Manolo tried to interrupt.

"And then you . . . you got through," he finished, smiling at Manolo.

Manolo set aside his swords and said, "I have to find La Muerte."

The Candle Maker whistled. "La Muerte? Sorry, you missed her, Manolo." He shrugged.

"Wait! You know me?"

"Yeah, man! We know everybody," the Candle Maker replied. He looked past Manolo. "We know Luis. Carmen. And Puddle." He paused, then asked, "How're you doing, Puddle?! High five!" He put his hand on the puddle to give it a high five. The puddle didn't move—it was just a puddle.

"Huh?" Luis gave Carmen a look indicating this guy was crazy.

Back in the museum, the kids were all stunned.

"Wow. That guy's nuttier than squirrel poop," Jane said.

The Candle Maker led the Sanchez family down a narrow hallway. "It's all here in the Book of Life! Wait, where are my manners? Come on in, y'all!"

Suddenly, the floor below them turned into a skull-shaped elevator platform. They went up and up, past a massive ceiling made out of clouds. When they arrived at the top, the Candle Maker moved aside so they could enter a large chamber lit by a billion candles. The ceiling was supported by four giant skeleton statues representing the four seasons.

"Welcome to the Cave of Souls!" he said. *"Mi casa es su casa."*

"Now, this is a cave!" Luis was impressed.

"You see all these candles? Each one is a life," the Candle Maker explained. He lifted his arms high and wide with a big grin on his face and formally introduced himself. "And I am your humble—yet strikingly handsome—Candle Maker!"

The Book of Life applauded its friend.

Manolo, Carmen, and Luis didn't know if they were supposed to applaud too. "I don't get it," Luis said.

"Wait. I didn't do the thing. I've got to do the thing. Watch this." The Candle Maker clapped his hands and hundreds of candles began to fly around them. "Amazing, huh?! This is our work! This is what we do." The Sanchezes looked on in awe at the floating candles and the godlike figure before them.

"Wow!" Luis exclaimed.

The Candle Maker pointed up and flew to a section of candles, all flickering in a breeze. "Look! That group— that's your town. And there," he said. "That's Maria." He grabbed two candles. One burned brightly. The other was unlit with a faint trail of smoke rising from it. "And next to her, Manolo." He raised one shoulder in a half shrug. "One aflame with life, the other—pfft. Kaput."

His attention was drawn to the Book of Life. "You see, as long as someone alive remembers you, you guys get to live in the Land of the Remembered." After checking a page, he exclaimed, "*Ay*, Cahuenga!"

"What is it?" Manolo asked.

"Chakal is on the march! With him comes the end of your town." The Candle Maker held up the open book, which showed Chakal and his men racing toward San Angel. Then the town burned away in an instant.

"We would all be forgotten," Carmen said sadly.

"Please, Candle Maker. Come on, help me get back," Manolo pleaded, a determined look on his face.

"I can't do that, Manolo," the Candle Maker said. But then the Book of Life tapped him on the shoulder and flipped open. *"Ay, caramba!"* The Candle Maker double-checked what he saw.

After a short conversation with the book, the Candle Maker told the Sanchez family, "Okay, okay. Look, you guys, the Book of Life holds everyone's story, but the pages on Manolo's life . . . they are blank."

The Candle Maker excitedly told Manolo, "You didn't live the life that was written for you. You are writing your own story."

CHAPTER 17

The Sanchez family gasped. "That's good?" Luis asked.

"So, does this mean you'll help me find La Muerte?" Manolo added.

The Candle Maker thought for a moment. "Well, I'm not supposed to interfere, but I may be able to bend the rules. Just a little." He raised his hands high and wide. "After all, it is the Day of the Dead. Right, book?"

The Candle Maker raised his hands again, and a waterfall in the cavern opened to reveal a hidden door. "Come on, let's do this. I'll take you to La Muerte." The Candle Maker stepped forward.

"I'm going alone," Manolo said, pushing past.

"Hold on, now—" the Candle Maker said.

Luis's head jumped into Manolo's arms. "Alone? Fine.

I'm going alone too, right next to you."

"Can I get a word in—" the Candle Maker tried to explain, but then Carmen said, "We should go."

Luis's hollow eyes glared at her. "We?! No. It's much too dangerous for a lady."

Ignoring him, Carmen made a dash for the waterfall portal and disappeared through it.

The Candle Maker tried once more to stop them all from going. "Actually, uh—" he started. "Hold on."

"No retreat." Manolo interrupted. "No surrender!" He leaped through the waterfall, carrying Luis's head with him.

The Candle Maker grabbed the Book of Life and told it, "I know, I know. I tried to warn them." He followed them all through the waterfall and deep into the Land of the Forgotten.

They fell. It seemed like forever. All Manolo could see were the spiked rocks and spires at the bottom of the cavern.

Somehow, they stopped inches short of the ground, floating momentarily in the air.

Clunk! Suddenly, the Book of Life caught all three of them at the last second. Manolo landed awkwardly on the book's face, while Luis hung by his teeth to the spine. Only Carmen stood upright, perfectly balanced.

The Candle Maker floated down alongside them as Luis clung to the book.

"Are you sure we're in the right place?" Luis asked.

"Of course you are! You Sanchezes need to look before you go jumping into magic waterfalls. What if you jumped into the wrong one? You might end up in Texas."

Luis's face lit up. "I think I died there."

A glow from the Candle Maker's body illuminated the area around them. There were dozens of destroyed buildings and pyramids. With a wave of his hand, the group continued to levitate away from the sharp rocks and gently landed on flat ground.

"Welcome to the Land of the Forgotten. Sad, huh?" As the Candle Maker said it, three crumbling black skeletons moved from the shadows. Their moans echoed with sorrow and grief.

"You poor things!" Carmen cried.

"What a bunch of sad sacks." Luis thought he was funny, but Carmen and Manolo gave him nasty looks. "What?! You were all thinking it," he said defensively.

"Grandpa!" Manolo groaned. "Come on!"

"You know what they forgot? They forgot to clean up! It smells like a dump!" Luis complained.

"Luis! *Cállate!*" Carmen shushed him one more time.

They walked on in silence a while longer, until the Candle Maker stopped. "There it is. Xibalba's castle."

Up ahead, a huge stalactite hung like a giant upside-down castle.

A carving of a two-headed serpent led to the castle's stairway. Manolo, Luis, Carmen, the Book of Life, and the Candle Maker crossed the moat of lava on a bridge shaped like a snake and entered the castle.

La Muerte was in the throne room, on a balcony over-looking the entire land.

Manolo quickly went out to join her. "La Muerte, I need a word with you, my lady."

She turned, surprised to see him there. "Manolo? But how did you get here? You're not forgotten."

He pointed back to his family and new friends. "I had some help."

"Hey there." The Candle Maker gave her a soft, loving look.

"Candle Maker! Carmen! And the head of Luis?" She snapped her fingers and Luis's missing bones flew into the room, reattaching themselves.

"Great, my arthritis is back." Luis moaned. Carmen shushed him.

Manolo was direct. "I know about the wager."

La Muerte was ashamed, but before she could apologize, Manolo said, "Xibalba cheated."

"He did what?!" Her eyes filled with fire.

Manolo pressed on, saying, "Yeah! With a two-headed snake!"

La Muerte's eyes narrowed and her jaw tightened. The ground began to shake from her anger. Her power filled the room.

"You might want to cover your ears right now!" the Candle Maker warned the others as La Muerte shrieked:

"XIIIIII-BAALLL-BAAA!"

There was a massive flash of lightning, and Xibalba appeared, holding two glasses and a fancy bottle. He smiled at La Muerte, clearly unaware of what was about to happen.

"Yes, my"—he spotted Manolo—"dear. Ooooh."

La Muerte was furious. "You misbegotten son of a leprous donkey! You cheated! Again!"

"I did no such thing!" Xibalba's words weren't convincing.

La Muerte reached into his beard and pulled out the two-headed snake.

"Oh, that. It has a mind of its own." Xibalba quickly turned it into a cane. "Or two." He laughed nervously.

"That is unforgiveable," La Muerte said. Each word was like a threat.

Xibalba wasn't backing down. "Oh, please! I never

sent that snake to Maria, and I never gave the medal to Joaquin—" He froze, realizing he'd said too much.

"What medal?" La Muerte asked in pointed tones.

Xibalba tried to correct himself. "The one I never gave him! Ever. At all. Never. Who is this Joaquin?" He was making a bigger mess, and he knew it.

La Muerte grabbed the whiskers on his face and tugged hard. "You gave Joaquin the Medal of Everlasting Life?"

In a tiny voice he said, "Yes?"

"Medal of Everlasting Life?" Manolo repeated. He hadn't heard of it.

"Whoever wears the medal cannot die or be injured," La Muerte explained.

"Tee-hee," Xibalba squealed.

La Muerte was ready to crush Xibalba into dust, when Carmen tugged on the base of La Muerte's dress. She asked, "Please, can you help me up?"

La Muerte levitated Carmen up so that she was right in front of Xibalba's face. With all the strength in her skeleton body, she smacked him three times.

She turned to La Muerte. "Thank you."

"Can I get a slap too?" the Candle Maker asked with a small grin.

"My son did not deserve this," Carmen said.

"Come on. I have to go back," Manolo demanded of Xibalba.

"It's only fair," La Muerte agreed.

Xibalba crossed his arms stubbornly.

"Please, Balby," La Muerte said, caressing her husband's skeleton face.

The entire Sanchez family was surprised. "Balby?" they repeated together.

"No. Never." Xibalba refused.

La Muerte's temper flared. "You better do this," she said through clenched teeth.

"No," he said again.

"Hey, how about a wager?" Manolo was willing to do anything to see Maria again.

That got their attention. "A wager?" the two rulers said in unison.

"If I win, you give me my life back."

Xibalba laughed at the suggestion. "You have nothing that I want," he said.

"I'll back Manolo," La Muerte put in. "If you win, Xibalba, you can rule both lands."

Manolo was determined. "You lay the terms. Any test you want, and I'll beat you." But Xibalba was still not convinced, so Manolo tried egging him on some more. "What?"

he goaded. "Are you afraid you might lose?"

"What are you doing, kid?" the Candle Maker asked. He couldn't believe what he was hearing!

Manolo ignored him. "Do we have a deal?" he asked Xibalba.

Xibalba smiled. "We have a deal. Now . . ." He moved inches from Manolo's face. "Tell me, boy, what keeps you up at night? What eats at you from the inside? What, do tell, is your worst fear?"

Manolo's eyes went wide as thunder crashed down from above. Xibalba's face stretched into a wicked grin. "Got it."

Xibalba snapped his fingers and Manolo immediately found himself in a massive bullring, dressed for a fight.

The Sanchez ancestors sat in the judge's box. Across from them Xibalba, La Muerte, and the Candle Maker looked on expectantly.

Xibalba shouted the rules. "Manolo Sanchez. You will have to defeat every bull the Sanchez family ever finished in the ring."

"That would be thousands!" Luis said with wide eyes.

"All at once!" Xibalba added, making it even harder. "If you complete the task, you will live again." Then there was the final decree. "And if you fail, you'll be forgotten. Forever."

"This is impossible. It can't be done." The Candle Maker shivered.

The gates around the stadium began to open. The ground shook like an earthquake. In an instant, the ring was filled with bulls.

There was only one thing to do. He had no choice. *"Vamos, toro! Venga!"* Manolo started to fight.

"Olé! Olé!" the crowd cheered.

"You can do it," Carmelo shouted.

Manolo managed to dodge the first few bulls, but they quickly began to overtake him as he was hit from all sides. It wasn't a fair fight.

Manolo kept getting hit over and over, until he finally fell to the ground.

CHAPTER 18

In San Angel, Ignacio and Luka came running out of the forest by the hill where Manolo had proposed. A bandit was chasing them.

Suddenly, Carlos stepped out from behind the tree and knocked the bandit out. "Are you two all right?" he asked the orphans.

"Chakal is coming! With a whole army behind him!" Ignacio announced, voice shaking.

"You boys warn the town." Carlos looked into the distance. "I will buy you some time."

A large group of *bandidos*, all holding torches, emerged from the darkness.

Carlos took out two swords and faced the men. "Who wants to go first?"

Chato let out a sinister laugh as the crowd of *bandidos* parted to reveal their leader, Chakal. Carlos sighed as he looked upon the bandit king.

Chakal was at least twice the size of any of his men. His bandits cowered in fear and reverence as he stepped forward and said, "I hate bullfighters."

"Then come and get some," Carlos roared. Then, raising his swords, he charged at Chakal.

In the Cave of Souls a candle flickered, then went out.

Skeleton Carlos arrived at the bullfight just in time to see Manolo get thrashed by the bulls. La Muerte gasped as she watched her champion being defeated.

Carlos leaned over and asked her, "What is happening?"

Carmen knew that beloved voice. "Carlos?" She rushed forward to hug him.

"Carmen!"

The Candle Maker shouted from the judge's box, "Manolo! Your father is here!"

Manolo managed to get to his feet. "Papa?"

With a heavy heart, Carlos shouted the terrible news to his son. "Chakal and his men are at the gates of San Angel!"

"You must hurry, my son!" Carmen said.

Stumbling forward, Manolo swung his cape, but now there weren't thousands of massive skeleton bulls. They were quickly combining into one gigantic monster beast. The beast roared so loudly that it blew the sombreros off the heads of the people watching.

"Man, this is a whole lotta bull," the Candle Maker remarked.

Unaware that the town was about to be attacked, Maria and Joaquin were getting married.

A single tear rolled down Maria's face as Father Domingo asked her, "Maria Posada, do you take Joaquin to be your husband?"

Maria said honestly, "Yes. For San Angel, I do."

"And Joaquin, do you take Maria to be your wife?" Joaquin paused. He looked at Maria, but she wouldn't meet his eye. General Posada sat in the pews, his foot tapping as he waited for Joaquin's reply. Joaquin knew that Maria was only marrying him to protect the town. *This wasn't how things were supposed to happen. Manolo was her true love,* he thought sadly.

"I—" Joaquin was about to speak, when the stained-glass window at the back of the chapel exploded into a million tiny shards.

Ignacio and Luka ran into the church. They announced, "Chakal is here!"

Joaquin took one look at the uniform he'd chosen to wear to the wedding. There were a lot of ribbons and awards pinned onto the jacket, but not what he needed. "My medal. It's on my other suit! I gotta go." He raced out of the chapel without looking back.

General Posada turned to his daughter. "But Maria, Joaquin is the only one who can defeat Chakal!"

"We can fight them together, Papa," Maria replied, tearing off her veil.

"Toro! Toro, venga!" Manolo faced the enormous monster bull. *"Venga, toro, venga!"* he called.

The bull charged. Manolo was surprised by its speed and when the bull smacked him, he was smashed backward into the arena wall.

"Get up and fight like a Sanchez," Luis shouted.

Beside them, Grandma Sanchez popped into the box, shook her head, and set down her knitting.

Luis turned around.

"Mama?! What are you doing here?" Luis asked.

"Meh." She shrugged. "Cholesterol."

*****

Chakal and his men crossed the bridge into San Ángel. He casually strolled through the town. His men followed, laughing as they destroyed everything in their path.

Maria and General Posada tried to calm the townsfolk.

Having changed out of her wedding dress, Maria was ready for battle, now wearing her traditional folkloric skirt.

"Everyone! Calm down and listen up!" She spoke to the crowd.

Pancho played tense music. Pepe whacked him with his hat.

"I know you're scared, but look around you. Do you know what I see?" Maria asked. The cowardly soldiers looked at each other nervously. "I see proud people ready to fight for their beloved town."

The nuns all held each other's hands while Father Domingo hid behind them.

Maria raised a sword in one hand and a pitchfork in the other. "And I see that inside each of you is a strength that cannot be measured." She glanced at the Rodriguez brothers. "Yes, even in you, Pepe." She stood up on her tiptoes and kissed Pepe on the cheek.

Pepe blushed.

Chakal and his men were getting closer to the church. Maria could hear them coming. She said, "This Day of the Dead will never be forgotten."

Father Domingo took off his priest hat and put on a colorful *lucha libre* wrestling mask instead. He was ready to protect his town.

"We will teach Chakal that he is messing with the wrong town." Maria raised her sword. Her hair and dress blew in the wind. She looked like a mighty warrior. "San Angel, I swear by those before us, we will not fall, not today."

General Posada stood by her side. Chuy howled like a coyote.

The town was ready.

Chakal and the *bandidos* now stood at the edge of the cemetery. "Medal!" Chakal shouted.

Maria and the general faced them, raising their swords. "Not today!" Maria said again. The townspeople cheered.

The battle was about to begin when Joaquin appeared— tall and proud atop his white horse. His medals glinted in the sunlight.

"Joooaaaquin!" He shouted his own name as he jumped off his horse. After a quick pause to straighten his sombrero, Joaquin joined the others at the front line.

"Where have you been?" Maria asked.

Before Joaquin could answer, General Posada said, "Thank goodness you are here."

Chakal's patience had run out. "You give me that medal. Right now!"

"All this is about a stupid medal? Are you kidding me?" Maria grabbed Joaquin's jacket and ripped it open, revealing the Medal of Everlasting Life.

Joaquin brushed her off, "Not now, Maria. It's Joaquin time."

With a giant leap forward, Joaquin rolled like a gymnast, getting close enough to Chakal to throw a heavy punch. But the bandit king took a swipe at Joaquin, knocking the medal to the other side of the cemetery.

The two stared at each other for a tense moment before Joaquin said, "Uh, hey, buddy, let's talk about this—" *Wham!* Before Joaquin could finish, Chakal landed a knock-out punch that sent Joaquin flying across the cemetery.

"Joaquin?!" General Posada called uncertainly.

The townspeople and bandits were all stunned at this change. The hero was down.

CHAPTER 19

"Toro! Venga, toro!" With unwavering resolve, Manolo faced the monster bull.

The bull charged, swinging its huge head at Manolo.

Manolo pulled off an unbelievable move and dodged away. The weight of the bull propelled it forward—and into the wall with a crash.

The crowd went wild!

"The beast is out!" Luis had never been so happy.

"Time to finish this," Carmelo said.

The whole arena cheered for Manolo as he hurried to get his weapons.

The swords lay next to his guitar. Manolo reached for them, but when he saw his reflection in the metal, he paused. With a quick glance up, he caught the eye of his mother in the stands. He nodded, then left the swords, grabbing his guitar instead.

The crowd gasped in horror.

"What is he doing?!" Luis was stunned.

Carmelo groaned.

But Jorge and Carmen saw something the others missed. They smiled as Manolo approached the fallen bull.

The bull was rising, snorting and angry, shaking off the dust from the arena wall. Fire came from his mouth and nostrils, like a dragon.

Manolo didn't waver. He took a deep breath and began to play. He made up the words to the song as he went along. Each word was an apology for the many years his family had wronged bulls in the ring.

Xibalba thought victory was his. The bull would never let the singer live like this. It was ridiculous.

The bull roared as he came close to Manolo. He raised his foot and snorted. But instead of stomping on Manolo, he slammed his hoof down on the ground nearby. When the dust settled, Manolo dropped to his knees in front of the bull.

The bull bowed in return.

Xibalba's skeletal jaw fell off from the shock.

La Muerte smiled as the crowd's cheers rose louder than ever before.

Very gently, Manolo set his hand against the creature's nose. The bull softly began to break up, crumble into dust, and float away like flower petals in the wind.

"He did it!" The Candle Maker jumped up with joy.

"Yes, he did," La Muerte agreed, grinning.

Xibalba grunted. "Yeah. I'll give him that."

Tears ran down Carlos's face as Carmen hugged him.

"But how did Manolo do this?" Carlos wondered.

"He's a Sanchez," his wife replied.

All of the Sanchez family rushed into the ring: Carmen and Carlos, Jorge and Carmelo, Grandma and Luis. It was a grand celebration.

Mary Beth told the children at the museum, "Xibalba had been wrong. Manolo's fear was never bullfighting."

Carlos told his son, "I told you a Sanchez man never apologizes."

"Papa, I—" Manolo began.

But his father cut in, saying, "But you just changed that. I should have been a better father. I am very sorry."

"No. You only wanted what was best for me," Manolo said.

"I am so proud of you, son," Carlos said, sweeping Manolo into a grand hug.

"I love you, Papa," Manolo told his father.

All the Sanchez ancestors hugged in one big family group.

Mary Beth said, "At that moment, Manolo conquered his greatest fear: being himself."

The crowd was screaming with excitement and calling Manolo's name. Their shouts and laughter would have gone on forever if Manolo wasn't in such a hurry to get back to San Angel. The ancient gods interrupted the applause.

"In accordance with the ancient rules," the Candle Maker began.

Xibalba and La Muerte continued together, "We give you life."

A bright light extended from their clasped hands.

Manolo shielded himself. Then suddenly, he began to rise. In a dazzling flash of light, he was transformed into a living man.

*****

Back in the Land of the Living the people of San Angel fought valiantly, but by sunset they had lost the battle.

Joaquin was lying beaten on the ground, pinned by several bandits. "Just spare them," Joaquin begged.

The Medal of Everlasting Life was lying at Chakal's feet. He picked it up and roared victoriously. "Yes! The medal is mine!"

CRACK!

The cemetery ground split wide open and smoke billowed out. Everyone was blown back by the force. The explosion sent the medal flying out of Chakal's outstretched hand.

Manolo appeared in the cemetery, landing in perfect form.

"What?" Chakal blinked at the figure standing before him.

"Manolo?" Maria didn't understand how he could be there.

He quickly walked to her and helped her up, then grabbed her by the waist and swept her into his arms. Manolo kissed Maria with all the love he had in his heart.

"But—" Chakal started.

Manolo put his hand up, shushing Chakal without even looking. Chakal was so caught off guard, he actually stopped talking.

Manolo took his time finishing his passionate kiss, then he let Maria go. Turning to Joaquin, he said, "Hold this for me, amigo." He tossed his guitar to his friend.

Raising two heavy swords, Manolo faced Chakal. "So, my father tells me you hate bullfighters."

Chakal had two swords as well. He raised them to match Manolo and spit on the ground. "I hate everyone," he snarled.

"Okay, let's do this." Manolo swiped a sword through the air.

"You and what army?" Chakal laughed.

"Yeah, man!" Chato started chuckling. The bandits laughed too.

That was when the army arrived: Skeletons Carlos, Jorge, Carmelo, Luis, Carmen, the Adelita twins, Uncle Chucho, and Grandma magically appeared.

The bandits didn't know what to do as the skeleton army formed a protective wall around the town.

The townspeople were stunned silent for a moment. Then they cheered.

Manolo turned to find La Muerte, Xibalba, and the Candle Maker all watching from the church tower. They looked very regal, powerful, and godly.

"It is the Day of the Dead, Manolo," La Muerte told him.

"And on our day we have a certain amount of . . ." Xibalba opened his wings.

". . . leeway," La Muerte said with a wink.

"Good luck!" the Candle Maker said.

"Thank you!" Manolo was grateful.

The ancient gods smiled and disappeared.

The ancestors surveyed them carefully. "The odds are against us," Jorge said.

Luis just smiled. "Just like we like it."

Joaquin and Maria, each with a sword, stood to the side of Manolo. The three amigos, united again, smiled at each other.

Maria raised her head and asked the boys, "No retreat?"

Manolo and Joaquin answered together, "No surrender."

The bandidos shrunk back, leaving Chakal on his own.

"He gonna do it now!" Grandma said.

"*Familia* Sanchez . . ." Luis led the charge. "*Al ataque!*"

Manolo, Joaquin, and Maria rushed toward Chakal. Chakal was so big, he easily took Manolo down and held Joaquin back.

Off to one side of the cemetery, Jorge sang opera as he conquered his own small group of Chakal's men. As he finished, he jumped away from the bandits, landing on his own tombstone with grace. He took a theatrical bow. It was a fabulous show.

The bandits dropped their weapons and armor—even their mustaches fell to the ground. One of them started clapping, hoping for an encore.

"Now your turn!" Jorge shouted at Carmelo. Carmelo fought his way through the crowd, spinning and leaping in time to the opera song Jorge sang. As he landed, the Medal of Everlasting Life flew through the air . . .

. . . and landed at the feet of the Adelita twins, who were fighting like warriors. They chattered as they took out bandit after bandit. "I was like, 'I think you look good, I like your hair.' And he was like, 'I like your hair—'"

The fighting stopped, as did the twin's chatter when the other sister noticed something important. "Are you wearing my boots?!" she asked in horror.

"They look better on me," the other said, looking guilty.

The girls ran off, chasing another *bandido*. "Come here, lover boy!" one said as her skirt knocked the medal away.

The medal hit Cuchillo square in the face. He smiled a devilish grin before a skeleton hand tapped him on the shoulder. Luis used his detachable head to distract the bandit while sneaking in some heavy punches from his detached body. His mustache got in some powerful strikes as well. The medal flew out of Cuchillo's hands, soaring above Carmelo and Grandma.

"Medal!" Carmelo said, launching Grandma into the air like a football. She caught it just in time and tossed it down to Father Domingo.

"C'mon! Go get 'em!" Sister Ana said as the nuns launched a masked Father Domingo. He body-slammed a bandit, causing the medal to fly back into the air again.

The medal at last landed in the hands of a cowardly soldier, who dropped it and ran away when Chato and his *bandidos* moved toward them.

"Chakal!" he cried. "We found the medal!" Chato did a little victory dance.

But then Chuy rose up from a tombstone behind him. Chuy called his pig friends, who came charging in with orphans riding their backs. "My comrades, unleash the fury," he oinked.

"*Qué?*" Chato didn't speak pig.

The stampede of orphans riding pigs trampled Chato and the bandits. The Medal of Everlasting Life disappeared into the cloud of dust.

"I'm done playing!" Chakal shouted as he launched into the air at Manolo and Joaquin.

"I got this," Joaquin said to Manolo.

"No, I got this!" Manolo shot back.

Taking advantage of the moment, Maria ran between her

friends and managed a double kick to Chakal's face. "Did I tell you I also studied Wushu?" Maria smiled as Chakal groaned.

Manolo and Joaquin were impressed, but Chakal was furious. "Enough!" he said, lashing out.

"Look out!" Maria shouted, pushing the boys out of the way just in time, but Chakal grabbed Maria and carried her away.

"Never mind, you guys, I got this," Maria panted sarcastically.

Chakal had her firmly in his grip, but she wasn't scared. She looked at him, annoyed. "Let go of me!"

"Get me the medal or your girl will pay!" Chakal threatened Joaquin and Manolo as he marched through the cemetery toward the church bell tower.

"Go find the medal," Manolo told Joaquin.

"But Maria—" Joaquin started.

"Find the medal. I'll handle this." Manolo took off after Maria.

"Got it." Joaquin cheered himself on. "Joaquin!"

Manolo chased after Chakal, stepping on fallen bandits as he ran. He climbed an outer wall of the church bell tower but he wasn't fast enough. Chakal was already near the top with Maria.

Finding a place to grip was difficult. Manolo slipped and fell several feet before Carmelo reached out of one of the church's tower windows and grabbed him.

"I save you, little Sanchez!" Carmelo spun Manolo around and tossed him like a shot put to the next window, where Jorge grabbed him.

"Good luck, Manolo," Jorge said before throwing him up one window to Luis.

"Kick his butt, grandson!" Luis tossed him past the next window, but no one was there.

Suddenly, Manolo began to fall. "Whoaaaa!"

Carlos reached out a window to catch him on his way down. "*Epa!* Where do you think you're going?"

"I have to get up there." Manolo looked at the very top of the tower.

"I was right. You have become the greatest Sanchez ever." Carlos tossed his son upward with all his skeleton strength. Manolo soared to the top of the spire where Chakal was with Maria.

Manolo slammed Chakal in the jaw. The giant dropped Maria and staggered back, hitting his head on the bell. Manolo caught Maria before she hit the ground. "Come on!" she said. "I had him exactly where I wanted!"

Chakal fell back, but managed to grab the edge of the

tower, crushing the brick under his fingers to dust. Chakal had a barrel of TNT. The barrel fell from the tower and slammed into a wooden cart on the street below.

BOOOM! The base of the tower cracked from the explosion.

Everyone looked up to find Manolo and Maria fighting with Chakal. "Care to dance, señorita?" Manolo asked.

"I thought you'd never ask," she said with a smile.

Bricks fell to the ground below as they fought. The tower tipped to one side. Maria and Manolo were sliding down—into the arms of their enemy. "Pretty good, *guitarrista*," she said to Manolo. "Now how about this!" She spun Manolo toward Chakal, knocking him off the edge as the tower came toppling down.

On the ground below, Joaquin was looking for the Medal of Everlasting Life when he saw that the tower above was about to fall on the nuns! "Watch out, sisters! Save yourselves!" he shouted, pushing the nuns out of the way. The tower landed all around them in a pile of dust and debris.

Maria was thrown from the tower, but Carmelo, standing atop a pyramid of Manolo's ancestors, caught her just in time. "Hi, Maria!" the ancestors chorused.

Chakal burst from the rubble, but his massive arm was stuck underneath the debris. Furious, he grabbed a torch and lit the sticks of dynamite that were strapped to his chest. "I'm taking this whole town with me!" he roared.

Manolo and Joaquin heard Chakal's threat, but they were tired from the fighting, and their swords were gone. Manolo was so weak from the fall, he could barely raise his head. How could they finish the fight?

Joaquin turned to look at the statue of his father nearby and smiled slowly. He grabbed Manolo and pulled him close. "No retreat?" he asked, putting an arm around his friend.

Manolo nodded. "No surrender." The friends gathered every ounce of strength they had left—and attacked.

CHAPTER 20

Manolo and Joaquin hurled themselves at Chakal, knocking him sideways from the rubble and into the space beneath the giant church bell.

"No . . . ," Maria cried as she watched her friends struggle to hold back the bandit king.

Under the bell, Manolo turned to Joaquin. "Don't stop fighting for what's right," Manolo said, sadly.

"What?" Joaquin began, but before he could say any more, Manolo shoved him from the bell with all his might. Joaquin went staggering over a barrel and fell a safe distance away from Manolo and Chakal.

Chakal, realizing the dynamite was about to blow, tried his hardest to escape, but Manolo held him back. "Don't forget me," Manolo said, locking eyes with Maria. And with that, Manolo kicked the last remaining support beam that held the bell to the tower. The bell fell with a loud clang, trapping Manolo, Chakal, and the dynamite inside it.

"Nooo!" Maria screamed.

BOOM! The dynamite inside the bell exploded, sending Joaquin flying across the cemetery. The muffled explosion shook the ground like a nuclear blast, but the heavy bell contained it. The bell toppled to one side as smoke billowed out.

The bandits knew that it was the end of their leader. "Chakal is defeated. Retreat!" they cried.

But Maria . . . she waited for the billowing smoke from the blast to clear away.

When she could see again, there was no sign of Manolo. Not at first, anyway, but moments later he quietly slipped out of a hole in the ground made by the explosion.

"Manolo?" Maria threw herself into his arms.

"It's me, *mi amor*," he said.

"But how did you survive?" She wondered, touching him again and again to make sure he was really safe and alive.

Manolo looked over to find La Muerte nearby. Xibalba and the Candle Maker were also there.

"Don't look at me," La Muerte said with a surprised smile.

Maria took the Medal of Everlasting Life off Manolo's back and showed it to Manolo. "Joaquin!"

Manolo turned. Joaquin's mustache was completely burned off, and he was wrapping a strip of cloth around his head to cover his left eye.

"You gave me the medal . . . ," Manolo said.

Joaquin stumbled over into his friend's arms. "I couldn't . . . let you pay for my mistakes," he said with a smile. The three friends hugged.

"You . . . ," began Manolo. "You were going to sacrifice yourself for me."

"The hero of San Angel," Maria added. She turned to Joaquin, touching his face lightly. "Are you all right?"

Joaquin stared at the medal for a moment with his good eye. "I have never seen more clearly," he said, throwing the magical medal to Xibalba—he didn't want it anymore. Xibalba caught it and nodded.

Joaquin turned to Manolo. "Time to cast our own shadows."

"And write our own stories," Manolo said.

Maria just rolled her eyes, giggling at the boys being so dramatic. "You guys," she said, laughing.

*****

Back in the museum, Mary Beth said, "And so Joaquin learned that to be a true hero, one must be selfless."

General Posada, Carlos, and Carmen made their way through the rubble toward the three friends.

"There is one more thing we need to do, son," Maria's father told Manolo.

That day, the living and the dead of San Angel joined together to celebrate the wedding of Maria and Manolo. The church was packed to standing room only. Everyone was there to see Father Domingo perform the ceremony.

Carmen and Carlos looked on with great joy, while the Candle Maker and the Book of Life helped officiate.

"Do you take Manolo as your husband?" Father Domingo asked Maria.

"I do," Maria said with all her heart.

"By the power vested in us by the Book of Life . . . ," the Candle Maker started.

"We now pronounce you, husband and wife. You may kiss—" Father Domingo hadn't finished when Maria leaned in and kissed Manolo.

"—the groom?" Father Domingo finished with a chuckle.

The townsfolk and their skeleton ancestors gave a joyful shout and threw sombreros in the air.

Skeleton Carmen said, "She's going to be a great Sanchez." Carlos was nodding with tears in his eyes.

"And today was a good Day of the Dead." The Candle Maker raised his arms in triumph. *"Ay-ay-ay!"*

High above the cemetery in the remains of the church tower, Xibalba and La Muerte looked on.

"Ah, well. I believe you've won the wager, *mi amor*. Along with my heart, all over again." Xibalba turned to face La Muerte.

"Ay, Balby." She faced him. It was like it had been when they were younger. Time faded and their love rekindled.

"I am so sorry, my love. You deserve better than me. I know that now. Will you ever forgive me?" Xibalba took La Muerte's hand.

"I do," she said.

Xibalba kissed her hand, then feeling empowered by the moment, swept her into his arms for a grand, romantic kiss.

✶✶✶✶✶

Outside the church Maria and Manolo were celebrating with the living and the dead.

"Husband, may I request a song?" Maria asked, a glimmer in her eye.

"As you wish, Mrs. Sanchez." He pulled out his guitar and began to play a beautiful song.

Everyone gathered around them, but instead of a circle, they formed a giant heart.

When the song was over, Manolo touched his forehead to Maria's, and they kissed.

In the museum, Mary Beth finished telling the children the story.

"And the world kept spinning and the tales kept turning, and new life was born and people passed away, but they were never forgotten. And the one truth we know, held true one more time: Love, true love, the really, really good kind of love, never dies."

The secret room at the museum flickered with candlelight. The children looked at Mary Beth, not wanting the story to end.

The museum guard wiped tears from his eyes. "*Caramba*. It gets me every time."

Mary Beth gathered the kids together. "Okay, kids, closing time." She pointed toward the exit. "Your bus should be outside waiting for you."

The kids left the room quietly, but by the time they got outside, they were talking excitedly about the story and Mary Beth and their time in the museum.

"A-may-zing," the goth kid said, rushing to the bus.

Through the bus window, Sasha waved at Mary Beth.

"Adiós, pretty lady!"

Mary Beth transformed into La Muerte, her true self. "Adiós, Sasha." She waved.

"La Muerte?" Sasha couldn't believe her eyes.

The kids ran to the bus window and stared out.

"La Muerte," Sasha confirmed.

The goth kid was so happy, he fainted!

The museum guard came to stand near his love. "You never cease to amaze me, *mi amor*." He transformed into Xibalba and took her by the arm. "Such passion."

"Anyone can die," she said. "These kids . . . they will have the courage to live."

Xibalba said, "I'll wager you are right." He pulled her into a passionate embrace.

The Book of Life closed its pages. "Hey!" the Candle Maker said. "Write your own story."